About Mitch's Kisses.

She once more felt his arms around her so tightly, and she remembered how it was to be against his strong body. She thrilled to the memory of having him so concentrated on just her, of how his hands moved on her back, petting her, rubbing her, pressing her against him. She was swamped with sensations, and it shocked her that she felt such excitement.

That brought her conscience to attention. She hadn't behaved very well. She had felt so marvelously attracted that she'd broken all the rules.

She didn't know Mitch. She'd only met him the night before. Yet she'd allowed him the kind of kisses no man had ever taken from her. She hadn't just allowed it, she'd helped him.

She ought to to be careful. If she was smart, she wouldn't conduct a dalliance with Mitch. She might flirt a little, but she would keep it light.

After those kisses? Now how was he going to accept light, sipping kisses when he was capable of kindling all her senses? Could she deny herself a repeat of that tempting, living fire, that remarkable ecstasy that licked along her nerves and trembled inside her, making her shiver with desire?

Well, she might allow just that much and no more. She could stop him.

Yeah? And who was going to stop her?

Dear Reader:

Welcome to Silhouette Desire—sensual, compelling, believable love stories written by and for today's woman. When you open the pages of a Silhouette Desire, you open yourself up to a new world—a world of promising passion and endless love.

Each and every Silhouette Desire is a wonderful love story that is both sensual *and* emotional. You're with the hero and heroine each and every step of the way—from their first meeting, to their first kiss... to their happy ending. You'll experience all the deep joys—and occasional tribulations—of falling in love.

In future months, look for terrific Silhouette Desire romances from some of your favorite authors, such as Annette Broadrick, Dixie Browning, Nancy Martin and Lass Small, just to name a few.

So go wild with Desire. You'll be glad you did!

Lucia Macro
Senior Editor

LASS SMALL
WRONG ADDRESS, RIGHT PLACE

SILHOUETTE *Desire*

Published by Silhouette Books New York

America's Publisher of Contemporary Romance

SILHOUETTE BOOKS
300 East 42nd St., New York, N.Y. 10017

ISBN: 0-373-05569-2

First Silhouette Books printing May 1990

Printed in the U.S.A.

LASS SMALL

finds that living on this planet at this time is a fascinating experience. People are amazing. She thinks that to be a teller of tales of people, places and things is absolutely marvelous.

One

If you were going south from Dallas toward San Antonio, Waco was about a third of the way. While Waco had escaped the mega-growth of Houston, it hadn't languished into a bypassed town. It had been there a while, so some of the buildings were brand-new, some were beautiful old treasures and some were in-between.

Among the treasures were proud houses that were being bought up and refurbished since the oil bust had made the housing market easier. One of those houses was being renovated by Mitchell Roads, a temporarily jobless oilcatter who was thirty, lean and muscled, with sun-blond hair and green eyes.

One rainy Wednesday evening, Mitch and the owners of the house, Nick and Lee Smith, were inspecting his progress. Lee said, "I wouldn't want to be solely responsible for the oil bust, but we're surely glad

you're free right now, Mitch, and can do this for us.
It's going to be just beautiful." The pregnant Lee
smiled at the plank walls, which were pale with a sta-
pled gauze base, waiting for the wallpaper.

His green eyes seeming to spill with humor, Mitch
looked at his friend's wife and slowly shook his head.
"The whole economy went under just so's I could be
available to do this house."

Nick mentioned, "Phil Temple accosted me today,
wanting to know just how much longer you'd be tied
up with us. Last week he bought that brown house on
the next street?" He questioned with his statement in
the do-you-understand way of Texans.

Mitch shook his head. "He's way down on the list.
Your friends appear to want these old houses, but
none of them wants to take the time to get the place
back to the original look all by theirselves. I suspect
that, after I've done all the dirty work, they'll come in
and smooth on a little paint and consider they've done
it all."

"Naturally," Lee agreed placidly.

Nick commented, "For an oil man, you don't do
too bad with a hammer and a saw."

"Muscle. It's all muscle." Mitch pulled up an arm
to show off, but he laughed.

"Don't work tonight, Mitch," Lee admonished.
"There's time enough."

Mitch looked at her nicely rounded stomach and
smiled. "Our projects are going to come out about
neck-and-neck. Anyway, I don't have nothing else to
do," he drawled in exaggeration.

Lee scolded, "You need to accept some invitations.
There're nice women in this town, and you should allow them to look you over."

"You know I'm shy."

Nick choked a little.

Earnestly Lee instructed, "It'd help you, if you'd just accept a dinner invitation now and then. You need to practice being with females. I know women are rather sparse out yonder where you've been, but you're in Waco now, and there are people here. Everyone wants to meet you. They all know the oil market is just temporarily down. There're women who would be *willing* to help spend your money when you get back up."

Mitch exchanged a telling look with Nick, before he told Lee, "I'll do that."

She sighed. "I'll be glad when all the painting's done, so I can be in here, too, and begin my part. I've finished the curtains for the front bedroom, and they're gorgeous! This house is going to have to be one of those for the House and Garden Walk. Mitch, you're doing such a beautiful job of it. But it takes—"

"—so *long*!" both men finished for her.

With virtue, Mitch then reminded Lee, "Anything worth doing—"

"—is worth doing well!" she shrieked and put her hands into her hair.

And the doorbell rang.

It was Mitch who automatically went to the door. Working there, he'd been in their house more than the Smiths had, and he simply... went... to... the door. And he opened it.

There stood a dream of a woman.

She had dark hair and blue blue eyes. She had a lovely figure inside that raincoat, he *knew* it. And she had a bare, ringless left hand.

She was shorter than he by about six inches. She was younger than he by about six years. And she was confused, which matched his reaction exactly.

They stared at one another. Actually he stared. She also looked at a piece of paper, then frowned beyond him at the inside of the house where she saw scaffolding, paint cans, ladders and obviously bare walls.

She said, "Uhh . . . I realize I'm a day early."

He loved her voice. He smiled encouragingly.

She asked doubtfully, "Is this 1201 Fremont?"

Mitch saw the cab driver waiting at the curb. "It's 1201 Premont with a '*P.*'"

Since she had expected a negative reply, her words were tentative: "Bed-and-Breakfast?"

"Oh, yes."

"Are you open?" Again she looked past him at the chaos.

"Come right in." Mitch stepped aside, turned toward the Smiths and flared his eyes at them in the most 'shut up' look they'd ever encountered.

They were so surprised that neither said a word.

"Sit here," Mitch said as he cleared a sander off a high stool. "Let me take your coat. I'm Mitch Roads. These are friends who are visiting. The Smiths. This is . . ."

"Linda Parsons. I made reservations."

"Right. I'll just go help the driver get your things inside out of this nice sprinkle."

Linda looked a little surprised. "It's raining."

Mitch nodded once to acknowledge that, gave the Smith couple a very compelling stare and went out the front door.

There was an awkward pause and, remembering Mitch's stare, Lee smiled as would a hostess and inquired, "Where's your home?"

"Dallas." She said it as if there could be no other place for a civilized person to live. She was from the Big D.

Lee went on politely: "Are you here just for the night?"

"No. I'll be here for a week or so. I don't much care for the idea of a hotel, but . . ." Linda looked around at the mess, still unbelieving. "He really isn't ready for guests, is he." She wasn't questioning. "I suppose I could find a hotel. I *am* a day early. But from the looks of things, I don't believe another day would help, too."

And Mitch came through the front door, emphatically putting down two cases. He reached back through the door for another, a big one. "Thanks," he said to an unseen person.

"Thanks," was the rumbling reply from the porch, then, "Hey. Much obliged!"

Getting off the high stool, Linda grabbed up her purse and said, "Oh, I forgot to pay him. I wasn't sure, you see, so I didn't want him to leave until . . . it didn't appear like . . . are you sure you can put up a guest?"

Mitch replied, "No problem."

The Smiths were fascinated.

Linda inquired carefully, "How much did you give him to make a cab driver exclaim that way?"

Mitch's face smoothed innocently as he replied, "Ten per cent."

"I must repay you, because this is on an expense account." She looked away and was modestly important.

"I got a receipt." He handed her the paper.

"Yes." She opened her purse and put it carefully with her return plane ticket in the airline folder.

"Have you had supper?" her host inquired.

Lee witnessed as Mitch smiled at Linda in a way that made Lee's scalp tighten. She glanced at her husband who looked bland. That alarmed Lee even more, so she blurted, "Mitch, Linda could stay the night with us."

Mitch turned his head normally and gave Lee a hooded look that figuratively nailed her thumbs to the wall and stuck her feet into a cauldron of boiling oil. He said a perfectly civilized sounding, "No need." And before anyone could say or object to anything else, he repeated, "Traveling all this way, you must be starved." Then he said to the Smiths, "Nice of you to drop by. Come back anytime."

Dismissed, Nick took his wife's reluctant arm and guided her dragging steps toward the front door.

Linda heard Mrs. Smith say to Mr. Smith, "'All that way.' It's only about a hundred miles."

And Mr. Smith replied, "You didn't count airport time."

"Yeah," agreed Mrs. Smith. Then her voice fading away, she said, "Mitch is so... shy."

Linda looked at Mitch and thought how difficult it must be for a shy person to run a bed-and-breakfast. She would have to be kind to him and not rattle his composure. "Is there a ba—May I wash?"

"You surely may. No hot water upstairs, yet. I'm putting in the upstairs water heater tomorrow. But I can carry up hot water from down here."

She asked doubtfully, "Enough for a bath?"

His eyes sneaked a quick look down her length and then glanced off to the side, as if he was considering her words and not her body. "It's no trouble at all. Let me show you your room." He indicated she was to precede him into the entrance hall.

There he picked up all three pieces of luggage, which bent even his wide shoulders. They came to the bottom of the grand stair as he told her, "I need to get the bed into your room, but that'll only take a minute or two. You can hang your clothes in the closet. Uh, did you happen to bring hangers?" he asked, as they reached the bayed landing with its to-the-ceiling bare windows and unpadded window seat.

"Yes," Linda replied efficiently. "There're never enough in a hotel, I've been told."

"First trip to Waco?"

"Yes."

"It's a great place. You'll enjoy your stay. A month, wasn't it?"

"Oh, no. We should be finished in a week, at most." But she was caught by the area at the top of the stairs. "This is a lovely upper hall." She gestured past the rail along the stair, to the tall landing windows and the view of the crowding trees beyond. "This area is the size of a full room." She looked around the empty space and at the bare wooden floor. "How are you going to use it?"

Lee had already told Mitch, so he could say quite easily, "As a sitting room so, uh, the guests have another place besides their rooms. Like you. You could come out here this month and—"

"Just about six days, altogether."

"Right. This week, and maybe work at the table when it's here. There'll be bookshelves along this wall—" he waved one hand vaguely "—a library table in the middle and two easy chairs over by the rail with a low table between them, and lamps. Sorta like another reading room. Or letter-writing place."

"Perfect. How many rooms do you plan to rent out?"

"There're eight bedrooms. I'll rent seven," he planned aloud, winging it. He nodded toward a doorway. "Here's where you'll be."

Linda looked inside the room to find it was starkly bare. She blinked once and slowly, with some care, looked up at Mitch's face.

As he put down her luggage, he said in an offhand way, "The wallpaper was going on tonight. I could still do it tonight, but you might be disturbed with me walking across your bed now and again. It'll get done tomorrow. I'll put the bed in tonight, and you'll be snug in here." He looked into her blue eyes and said it yet again, "It'll be finished tomorrow. Promise."

"I'm sorry to put you to all this trouble. But tomorrow's plane didn't get in until the afternoon, and I wanted to get started first thing in the morning."

"Really. It's a pleasure."

"I tried to call—"

"Oh, yes. Uh, our number's been changed." He held his breath to see if she would believe it.

"I'd better put it down." She opened her purse. "I thought your brochure was excellent."

"Oh? Which one did you get?"

"This one." She took it from the airline folder. "See? Why, it does say *F*remont Avenue."

"Oh, yeah." He acted as if he'd just remembered the mixup. "That was the trial run, and the printer got it wrong. We're correcting it." Oh, what a tangled web we we—"You freshen up, and I'll go down and fix us something to eat."

"Does dinner really come with bed-and-*breakfast*? I thought only breakfast."

His hand moved toward the window. "It's sprinkling outside."

She corrected: "It's a gully-washer."

"You're right. The March rains. They'll make the bluebonnets bloom beautifully in another week or so. Waco is particularly pretty the first of April."

"I'll take your word for that."

"Supper'll be ready shortly."

"That's really very kind. Thank you."

"My pleasure." He smiled like a man who knew exactly what he was doing.

She gave him a cautious, quizzical look.

His own look turned innocent and earnest. "You've got a choice. Microwaved chicken and broccoli, spaghetti and meatballs, enchiladas and rice with beans, or hamburgers."

She tilted her head and chose, "Enchiladas."

"It's always a pleasure to meet an intelligent woman."

He showed her the bath and, with the door barely closed after her, he went to another room. There he tore the sheets and blankets off the only bed—his bed—in the whole house, and carried the queen-size mattress into her room and propped it against the wall. Then he went for the box spring and slid that on its side down the hall. Finally he fetched the metal rack that kept the bed up off the floor.

Then he went to Lee's already stocked linen closet, ruthlessly untied the neat ribbons that held the new linens, took out sheets, pillowcases, blankets and a spread. He was efficiently making up the bed when Linda came into the room.

"You do that very well."

"Scoutmaster," he explained.

"You had one?"

"I was one. Out in West Texas. Have you ever tried to teach Indian children how to get along in the rough? I learned a lot."

She laughed and relaxed. A shy scoutmaster sounded harmless. "Have you other guests coming soon?"

"You're my first," he replied in all honesty. He went for the only two pillows in the house, brought them back and slid them into new cases. He placed them at the top of the bed, smoothed them with suddenly slow hands, then efficiently flipped the coverlet over the mass, and Linda helped adjust it on the bed.

He stepped back and smiled at the bed, before he said to Linda, "There you go. All set."

"Yes." She saw a big bed in an empty room and wondered where she was supposed to put her non-hangable things.

"You can use the cupboards and the counter in the bath. Okay? I'll use the one downstairs."

He'd be in this house with her. She slid a side-glance at him. He was just gorgeously male. She dipped a quick glance down him. Very male. Her cheeks heated a little, and she straightened her back. Of course that poked her bosom out so she slumped a bit. She would be alone with him, all night long. "Did your wife choose the colors?" She blushed scarlet for such a question, but she did need to know.

"I'm not married. You?"

"No. What made you get into the bed-and-breakfast business?"

"I sort of just...seized the opportunity." He smiled guilelessly. "Come down and watch me cook. You can unpack later."

In the dining room, Mitch retrieved two carpenter's sawhorses and two wide planks for a table. He got two ladders and put a plank across the second steps, from one to the other, for a bench. She was quite charmed.

The floor was covered with paint-spotted canvas, on which were some sawdust and curls of wood shavings. There were pieces of wood helter-skelter in a bushel basket, which he lifted and carried into the living room.

"May I help?" She opened out her hands in a willing way.

He eyed her narrowly. "How are you at salads?"

"Brilliant." She lifted her eyebrows and smiled a little.

"You're hired." He led the way into the kitchen. It was like the bathroom, almost finished, and very little more work was needed. Even there, the floor was natural wood. The cabinets and counters had been redone, again in wood. It had been completely renovated. Lovely. Linda smiled.

He opened the giant double-refrigerator and began to set out salad things: lettuce, an onion, cheese, a tomato and a bottle of vinegar and oil. He found two bowls in a cupboard and gave her a knife. "Be careful. It's really sharp."

"What do you feed your guests for breakfast?"

"Doughnuts and coffee?"

She hesitated.

"Are you bacon and eggs with toast, or are you wheat germ, yogurt, brewer's yeast and grains?"

"A little of both?" She, too, questioned with statements.

"You got it."

He did have two plates, both of which were in the sink. He washed them quickly, along with the forks and knives and two of the glasses. She didn't comment.

He wiped the two-plank table with wet paper towels, then went outside and returned with a rain-wet budding wisteria branch, which he put in a discarded beer bottle. He set that on their contrived table, then folded paper towels as napkins. He was busily efficient and he intrigued her. He made no excuses; he simply used what was at hand.

"One or two dinners?" he inquired with his head in the freezer half of the refrigerator.

"One is plenty."

He put three dinners into the microwave and punched in the time. "How's the salad coming?"

"Excellent."

"I like your attitude of confidence." He challenged, "How do you know I'll think it's excellent?"

"How could you not?"

He raised his eyebrows and teased back, "How could I not?"

"You may taste it. It is only excellent instead of perfect because to be perfect it would have to set a while to be imbued with the essence of the dressing."

"Oh, yes." As he said the two words, he put his head way up and then put his chin down to his chest in one solemn nod. He grinned at his guest, delighted with her. She could tease a little.

He thought that it wasn't at all necessary that she be the perfect woman. She could just sit in a chair and let him look at her—that would be more than even a choosy man could expect. But she could talk and move just like ordinary folks. He had noticed that she tended to be a little literal, but if she could also be teased with it ... No, that would be asking too much.

He considered that she could adjust well. Look how she'd handled this whole situation. Any other woman would have left. Linda had ridden it all out; and here they were, about to eat fast food on a plank table, sitting on a board bench. She was a treasure.

Treasure? Was she a treasure ... hunter? Had she heard he was an oil man? He gave her a cynical glance and saw that she was critically taking a bit of lettuce from the salad. He watched her mouth open to take in the bit. Then he saw her tongue lick her lip as she raised her head and narrowed her eyes to concentrate.

Not even aware of him, she moved in a quickened, satisfied way, licked her two fingers with dispatch, then washed them at the sink. The tasting had been unconsciously done; she wasn't deliberately luring him.

The buzzer sounded and their meal was ready. He slid the dinners onto an oddly cut piece of discarded plywood and carried them into the dining room. She followed with the salad.

"Beer or wine?" He gave her the choice.

"Wine?"

"Sorry. I'm out of candles."

She breathed the wood smell of the partly done room and said, "This is just right."

What a woman. My God, what a woman. Or was she? In the kitchen he rinsed out a beer bottle and filled it with wine, taking it back to her. "Be careful of the crystal," he said of the beer bottle. "Try this. It is wine."

She sipped carefully, smiled, and her eyes danced with sparkling humor. "Fine."

He would marry her. If she could be this way for a whole week, he absolutely would marry her. "Why are you in Waco?"

"I'm here to train the staff in computer use at Stewart's Hardware and Supply. Our company sold them the system."

"Sounds impressive."

She looked around at the work being done in that house. "Expertise takes many avenues."

"Well said!" Maybe she was older than twenty-four.

She recognized that his English varied. He sometimes spoke roughly, as would a field man. Then again, he spoke in a way that showed he knew how to speak well. Interesting. Not an ordinary man.

He looked over at the chili dinner on her cardboard platter. "Is that enough?"

"It's just right. This is nice. A picnic in a house. You were very kind to include me."

He nodded to acknowledge that, then asked her, "In your job, how often do you have to go out of town?" He found he was a little jealous of other bed-

and-breakfast places. He wondered who ran them and how they had looked at Linda.

She admitted, "I've never before been outside the city limits."

"Of what?"

"Dallas."

He thought she said "Dallas" as if that was the only rational reply, where else could anyone possibly live? People in Dallas thought that way. It was like New York. The citizens of those towns tended to be surprised when they got out into the countryside and found other people didn't pay much attention to them. Mitch said seriously, "Well, it is just a little wild and woolly clear down here in Waco. Want me to sleep across your doorway and protect you from marauding cowboys and Indians?"

"That won't be necessary. One of the requirements in my position is knowing how to take care of yourself."

With a strange inner intensity, he instantly inquired, "Had to use that talent lately? At all?"

"Not so far. I've been a little disappointed. I'm really good."

"I could lay a mat and give you reason," he offered in an accommodating helpfulness.

"Never mind."

"Do men who... come on to you make you mad?"

"It depends on how they handle the approach. Some men are very clumsy, some are insulting and some are so charming that it's almost hard to refuse."

"But you do? Refuse?"

"I'm not a sleep-around."

"Me either."

She rose and picked up her cardboard platter. "Since you cooked, I'll clear away."

He scoffed at her generosity, "Two forks, two knives, and two beer bottles. Big deal."

She looked down her nose and retorted, "And two salad bowls. You forgot them."

He laughed in his delight of her. "With two salad bowls, I'll have to help you."

"Look at it rain! God doesn't think you're building an ark, does He? You haven't been sending the wrong signals, have you?"

"If I get word, I'll sign you on."

"How kind." Then with emphasis, she declared, "I don't do ark floors."

"Ah. Well. I'll have to think of something... else... for you to do."

His tone lay a touch of suggestiveness onto the silence. She gave him such a practiced, quelling side-glance, that he thought she might indeed be older than twenty-four. He followed her into the kitchen.

God couldn't think he was building an ark, because Mitch hadn't mentioned he'd been working in carpentry, except for one nail and a stubborn board. But he just might start mentioning Linda Parsons. Not yet. No one was that perfect. She had to have flaws. He followed along into the kitchen carrying the wisteria centerpiece in the beer bottle. "Tell me your biggest hate."

"Liars."

He was taken aback. She hadn't even hesitated. She'd spat it out like something nasty. And he had lied to her. He'd said that was his bed-and-breakfast brochure. He'd said this was the place where she was registered. How strict was she? Did she make exceptions to men who were bemused by her?

In the silence, she dropped her views: "You have no idea how inventive men can be. Maybe you do. Do you lie to women?"

"Uh...well... You see there *are* times when a man just *can't* tell the unvarnished truth. There are times when he *has* to bend the facts...just a tad. Now, you can't tell me you've never told any woman that she was a good cook when you weren't able to stomach the mess she'd served you."

"I've said I wasn't hungry."

"And you were starving."

"Well...yes," she admitted grudgingly.

"We'll get along."

She instructed him sternly, "Fibbing to people so you don't hurt their feelings isn't a lie."

He nodded once to indicate he understood the difference, but he thought to himself: She's a stickler. Stubborn.

He watched her bottom as she went to the refrigerator and bent over to put the rest of the salad inside. A stubborn woman wasn't unpalatable. It would depend on what she was stubborn about.

As she straightened and turned back, unaware, he said, "I have some errands. I have to pick up your door key." And several other things.

She assured him, "I don't expect you to entertain me."

She was being kind. He thought of ways he could entertain her and became restless. "You're perfectly safe here. There's no one anywhere around."

"No one?" Her eyes widened just a little.

"I'll be here. Don't worry. And I'll be right back. You can lock the doors after me."

She looked out into the darkening rainy evening. "Do you have newspapers and some gummed tape?"

"I can get some."

"I noticed there aren't any drapes or shades. I'd like to tape some paper over my windows."

A modest woman. A young, nubile, beautiful sacrificial maiden. He smiled. "You got it."

Two

Linda watched Mitch go off the big porch with effortless male grace and dash across the rain-swept, unkempt yard to his car. It was a low-slung green one that looked like a predator. Would a shy scoutmaster drive such a car? Only wicked predatory men drove such automobiles. Linda felt a quiver of something or the other slither through her body in a very pleasantly shocking way.

Thoughtfully she turned from the locked front door and looked back into that big house. The stairs rose to the right. Ahead at the far end of the hall a fireplace waited to be used. Through the double doors to her left was the library. Farther down the big entrance hall was a second set of double doors that led into the middle room—the living room. Behind that was the dining room where they'd had supper. The kitchen was behind the hall's far wall, and there were other rooms on beyond the kitchen.

It was a big house. A very quiet house. It was getting dark. She reached confidently over to one of the switches by the front door, but the switch only clicked. She tried the whole bank of five switches, but none worked. In the dimming evening light, she went into the other rooms and found none of the other switches worked, either. The kitchen lights snapped on efficiently.

But the hall lights didn't. She went cautiously up the stairs and sought her purse, which held a small hand flashlight. None of the bedroom lights worked, but in her flashlight's beam, she saw the discarded sheets and blanket on the floor in one empty bedroom.

She figured it out. He'd moved his bed into her room. He *really* hadn't been ready for a guest. He'd have to sleep on the floor. There wasn't even a sofa. That was too bad.

She went back and looked again at her bed. It was queen-size and big enough for two. Now if this was a Romance, and the heroine and hero were in that empty house, she would offer to share her bed... platonically. And they would lie there awake and breathing heavily until Mother Nature would overwhelm them, and they'd meet in the middle and make mad, passionate love. Right? Wrong.

She sought through the rest of the subtly echoing, listening rooms and found two other baths still waiting for fixtures. The lights in her bath worked. That was some relief to her.

She had always been a little afraid of the dark. For that very reason, she'd chosen the more family-feeling of a bed-and-breakfast over a solitary hotel. Now she doubted her choice. A hotel could never feel this isolated. If she screamed, who would hear her?

From the upstairs hall, she looked down the darkened stairs, then beyond the tall landing windows to the newly leafed tree limbs, which moved restlessly. Her imagination was convinced they were trying to get inside. The killer trees.

She wondered how long Mitch would be gone? What if he went to a motel? He needed to sleep, and he had honored her reservation by giving her his bed. Maybe he'd just go to his friends, the Smiths. And she'd be there in that big, dark, silent house, all night, all alone.

She heard a scratching sound and shivers coldly touched the backs of her shoulders. Lights swept across the front of the house as a car turned into the driveway. Linda froze at the top of the stairs. Who would it be?

A car door slammed, footsteps leaped up the wooden front steps and seemed to thunder across the wooden porch floor...to the door. A key was fitted into the lock and a man entered. He flicked the switches by the door and said, "Damn. Linda?" he yelled up the stairs.

"Mitch?" She started down the stairs with the tiny flash showing her way.

"Who else? You okay? Sorry about the lights. I'll fix the fuses. I keep them off so I don't accidentally run into any live wires—"

"Live."

"—when I'm working in the walls. There's no danger. There aren't any wires to step on or to touch. I brought back the Waco paper. Here. You can read about all that's happening. You'll see we're even nicer than Big D. I'll fix you a little fire in the fireplace, and you can read the paper before you tape it on the windows. It's easier to read, holding it, instead of having to crane your neck to read the paper taped on the windows." He chatted because he realized she'd been scared, alone there in the dark. "Are you all right?"

"Yes."

But she was glad to see him. She stood closer to him than she had that evening. It pleased him, in a way, but it also touched his compassion. She pretended to be so self-sufficient, but she was vulnerable. Well, she had nothing to fear—he'd take care of her. And he smiled in self-derision. In this day and age, what could threaten her?

After screwing in the fuses that she'd need, Mitch efficiently made a small fire for her and it flickered warm lights in the empty library. He had a lawn chair that he pulled close to the fire, and there was a table lamp sitting on the floor. He turned it on, and the light from below threw eerie shadows up onto his face, making him look strangely ominous.

That was the trouble with imagination, and hers worked rampantly. With Mitch there, the scratching sound had stopped. The wind was still blowing so the scratching sound wasn't from the tree branches moving against the house. Linda sat down with the paper, and Mitch went back to his errands.

He went to Wal-Mart, bought a sleeping bag and added an inflatable mattress. He'd get a bed tomorrow. He could hardly carry in a bed tonight. She might think she'd inconvenienced him.

He bought more food at the grocery, with eggs and bacon and cereal. Orange juice—she probably loved it. Then milk, cookies and fruit. Bread. All the things

he thought she might like. And candy. He remembered the old saying about candy being dandy, but that
liquor was quicker. So he bought some nice wines, and
he smiled as he bought two crystal wineglasses.

She was still by the fire when he returned. He
thought she was a little bug-eyed. Although she acted
as if nothing were wrong, she was obviously relieved
that he'd returned. "How about some cookies and
wine?"

"All right." She got up immediately, taking one
grocery bag from him and following him into the
kitchen.

He went out for the rest of the bags, and Linda met
him at the front door. She put up one hand to stop him
and put a finger to her nice lips for him to be quiet.

He whispered, "What's the matter?"

She whispered back, "I hear something."

"What?"

"Shhh. It stops when you talk."

"It's probably just a mouse."

"A *mouse*?" she squeaked.

He guessed, "You don't like mice?"

She looked at him as if he'd taken leave of his
senses.

He was sure: "You don't like mice."

"We don't have mice in Dallas."

And he had the gall to laugh. He went past her with
his sacks of groceries and said, "Just stomp your feet
when you walk, and remember that you're bigger 'n
them."

She followed him like his shadow, and he loved it.
There's nothing that makes a guy feel more manly
than a woman who is afraid . . . when he isn't.

He sorted through the groceries, putting them away. She washed the fruit, and he found a basket to put it in. But before he could do that, she snatched the dusty basket away and washed it, too. She was tidy.

They took their cookies to the living room by the fire, and he sat on the floor. Looking at her, he lifted his wineglass and said, "To bed-and-breakfasts." His eyes glinted in the firelight.

Mitch's toast appeared to amuse him unduly, and she gave him a measuring look. She wasn't a drinking woman, but she sipped the wine. It was cool on her tongue and warmed her insides. How strange.

He asked, "Did you get the paper read? What's going on?"

"There's a Wind Festival this Sunday! I've never heard of one. It sounds marvelous. Kites, sailboat races, Frisbee contests, soap bubbles, a wind-instrument concert, all the things that use wind. How charming. How clever."

"I've never been to one, either," he commented with interest. "I'm pretty new here. We'll have to go."

"Where have you lived?"

"Out in West Texas. I'm a roustabout. The oil fields are mighty empty right now, but the wells will come back."

She lectured, "People need to diversify as much as companies. Anyone needs to have alternatives. Oil is a tricky business. You're very wise to have this other skill." She gestured to indicate the renovation of the house.

"Do you know, once when the heads of OPEC met, along with them was a Texan? The U.S. government was indignant that a private citizen would meet with heads of state about oil prices, like he was a head of state, too. But Texas has privileges the U.S. of A. doesn't always recognize or understand.''

"Was it you who went?" she wanted to know.

"No. Hardly."

But he'd smiled and tried to hide it. Who was he? "Rhodes. Are you of the South African Rhodeses?"

"No. Our name is spelled like the tracks you follow with vehicles. I was called Rocky, until I grew up. I'm Mitchell Roads.'' He looked at her, but she didn't blink so she'd never heard of him.

She told him seriously, "I know how inconvenient and disruptive my coming a day early has been for you. I just want you to know how much I appreciate your courtesy."

"It's my pleasure. As my first guest, you merit all sorts of privileges. Name it—you got it.''

She thought his tone was a little sassier than an inn host's should be. It was as if he invited her to make all sorts of...demands on him. And he sat and waited expectantly, as if she might do just that. Like saying, Let's go upstairs and climb up on that bed and test the springs. She said, "I really need to unpack. Tomorrow will be a long day. Mitch, where will you sleep?''

"In another room?"

So she wasn't supposed to know that she had his bed. She didn't pursue that; it might lead to blunders on her part. She then simply said, "Good night," as she should have in the first place.

He got up and sort of followed her to the foot of the stairs. It wasn't a deliberate following but rather as if he had been drawn along behind her. Then he stood there and watched her go up the stairs. He made her feel very safe, escorting her like that.

He was watching her bottom move as she climbed the steps. He thought how female she was.

At the landing, she glanced back. He was still there, waiting for her to be safely in her room. She smiled down at him. "Good night." Her tone was grateful.

The sound of her voice floated down the stairs and curled into his body and concentrated uncomfortably. Now how was he going to fill the evening? He couldn't hammer or saw. He could put up wallpaper. But not in her room.

He went out to the car and brought in the thick sleeping bag with the inflatable mattress. He carried them up the stairs to his room and laid them out in some disgruntled disgust. She would be more comfortable. Think of lying on her... with her round breasts and curvy hipbones, her grasping hands and strong, hugging thighs. His eyes closed against the erotic tide that swamped him and his mouth opened so that he could breathe.

This woman was the only one he had ever yearned to tempt his body. He'd known her for five hours. Linda Parsons was a witch. He'd never felt such sudden, avid interest in a woman since he was sixteen.

Why did women need preliminaries? He already knew they ought to be up on that bed, thrashing around and pleasuring themselves. And she acted as if he was her guardian angel, for Pete's sake. And she was afraid of mice?

Too bad he'd been civilized.

But she almost wiped out all traces of those civilizing lessons with three words. She came back to the stair landing and leaned over the rail in order to see him. She was wearing a pink wrapper that, with her dark hair, made her look like a chocolate-topped confection, ready to be eaten. The three words she said were, "About that bath..."

He moved to stand below her, looking up as she leaned there, and he felt like Romeo. Juliet had been a receptive child-woman. Linda was full grown. He said, "Want your back scrubbed?" He slid his hands into his jean pockets.

"No. You said you could provide hot water? Please."

"Oh, yes." He sighed, stretching his shoulders up as he pushed his hands deep into his pockets, then he smiled up at her. "Coming, right away."

He went to the storage room behind the kitchen and fetched a metal bucket, which he filled at the hot-water tap. He then set it on the stove to boil. It didn't take long.

He carried the bucket upstairs, saying, "Watch it. This is dangerous." He thought it was possible that she could consider the danger was solely in the bucket.

She stepped from the room, out into the hallway, and he realized she didn't have on anything under that pink robe. She had the lapels modestly folded high under her chin, but her body shape was apparent under the clinging soft wool. He thought maybe he could heat the water all by himself.

She had cold water running into the tub, and he poured in the boiling bucketful. He watched it swirl into the cold water and he thought about her bare body sitting in the tub. He shook the bucket for the last drop and said, "There you go. Enjoy."

He didn't allow himself to look at her again, but went quietly down the stairs and looked around for something physical he could do that didn't involve Linda.

He was painting when he heard the scratching. Stocking footed, he went around looking, and he found a big, gaunt, bedraggled black tomcat on a windowsill under an overhang outside the storage room behind the kitchen. The cat was asking to come inside.

Feeling a fellowship to any lone and abandoned creature, Mitch invited the cat in; and predictably the cat hesitated before it agreed to come inside.

The cat looked around the unfurnished house in a disapproving way, accepted milk with a beaten egg over crumbled bread, and prowled in a head-swivelling but straight line to the fireplace. The cat inspected the dying fire and turned to bend a critical and commanding look on Mitch.

Recognizing a fellow male who liked things his way, Mitch obediently added wood to the small fire. With an audible sigh of resignation, the tomcat began to repair the weather damage to his fur.

Mitch was in a particularly sympathetic mood, so he fetched a towel and got the cat started. Then he went back to his painting while the cat finished the fur job. The next time Mitch looked the cat was sound asleep but in a tight ball, ready to waken and move at the same time. The cat had obviously been roughing it for some time and had forgotten about a sprawling, re-laxed sleep.

Mitch considered that he had two nervous visitors in his care. Linda, who didn't like the dark or mice, and a tomcat who had been on his own. Mitch shook his head. He didn't like cats, but there was one on his hearth, uh, the *Smiths'* hearth. And upstairs was a woman who thought Mitch was her protector.

Mitch worked until he could sleep, so it was almost two in the morning. He showered in the downstairs bath and put on fresh underwear. He put some more chunks of wood on the fire for the cat, replaced the screen and went barefooted up the stairs.

Her door was closed. He did hesitate there but went on to his own room. He slid into the sleeping bag and stretched his tired muscles. Then he got up, rummaged through his closet to find his alarm clock, set it for six o'clock and went to sleep.

It went off two minutes later and he scowled at the clock, but it really was morning. It was still raining and dismal daylight was about to creep in. He tried to stretch but was hampered by the damned cat who was pushing him clear over to the side of the sleeping bag. The cat was dead to the world, out cold.

It amazed Mitch. In that house were two creatures who trusted him. Neither should.

He unzipped the bag and slid out, not disturbing the cat. He put on jeans and a pullover, socks and sneakers and went downstairs where he organized breakfast. Then in the time he waited for her to get up, he stripped the tape off the windows he'd painted.

At seven, he went up the stairs with a cup of coffee and tapped on her door. He heard the sheets whisper as she moved; then the sound stopped dead as she realized where she was.

He tapped again. "Linda? You didn't ask for a wake-up call. What time do you want to get up?"

From the other side of the closed door, she exclaimed, "Why, it's seven o'clock already?"

"Yes, ma'am, it surely is. How about some coffee?"

"Don't come in!"

"Heavens to Betsy, no. I'll leave it in the bath. Okay?"

Her sleepy muffled voice said, "Thank you."

And in a perfectly civil way he replied, "You're welcome," just as if he meant it. And he went downstairs muttering about her saying "Don't come in," as if he'd been planning to burst through the door and jump her. Of course, he had turned the knob, but the door had been locked.

She didn't trust him.

Her voice had sounded so sleepy. He bet she was all warm and tousled, lying up there in his bed, stretching, her naked body supple and smooth.... She was probably wearing an iron body-protector riddled with rivets. Yep. That was probably what she wore to bed.

The cat came into the kitchen and exchanged a look with Mitch. Then the cat came over in a lordly way and rubbed its chin against Mitch's leg. Mitch growled, "I know about the marking. On PBS I watched a whole hour on cats, once, when I broke my leg and had to stay put for a while. So I know you're not acknowledging me as your master, you're marking me as your slave. You expect me to open doors and hand out food and take care of you."

The cat looked up at him. Mitch knew the cat understood him exactly and humor lurked in the depths of those green eyes.

"So you have green eyes. That does not make us kin. All you have to do is be sure Linda isn't scared by a mouse. Got that?"

The cat lowered his head in amusement, or boredom. He walked over and looked back, requesting the door be opened.

"At least you're housebroken. You get to keep your skin."

The cat ignored the man.

Mitch was whipping eggs for an omelet when the cat yowled to be back inside. Mitch put down the bowl and went to the door. "A simple scratch on the window would have done just fine. Cut the yowling."

Linda hesitated in the doorway. "Yowling?"

"Not you. The cat."

"You have a cat? My goodness, what happened to him? He looks moth-eaten."

"He's been roughing it. Give him a little time and he'll be sleek again and on his way. He's a hobo cat. A wanderer. How did you sleep?" . . . in his bed.

"I didn't hear anything but the leaves in the rain, and the sound lulled me to sleep like a lullaby."

She'd slept while he'd had to work his tail off until 2:00 a.m. before he could sleep, and she felt safe with him. But not too safe. She'd locked her door.

She was asking, "Did you sleep?"

"Like a rock," he lied. He'd been besieged by erotic dreams all night long. Well, during the four hours he'd slept.

"Omelets? Great. I'm starved."

She carried things to the dining room, bright and cheerful and a little excited.

"Where exactly are you working?"

"Stewart's Hardware and Supply."

He said, "I've read something about computer viruses. The bad guys put in commands that multiply or that wipe out information."

She agreed, "A company might fire someone who then takes revenge. Or the main computer is hooked up to a modem, the telephone connection that can spread a virus, or someone uses pirated software that's deliberately infected. It's all a hassle.''

"You know computers that well?" He was amazed.

"Yes," she replied shortly.

So she had run into disbelief before. That wasn't any surprise. She looked so fragile and precious that no one would ever wonder if she had a brain, too. But he admitted such an attitude from men could be insulting to such a woman. "I can use a computer."

"Good for you." It was a neutral reply.

"They're magic."

With the use of those particular words, he hit a common bond with her. "Aren't they, though. I am just amazed at all that can be done with them. They really are magic that is carefully constructed by good brains.''

"Can you detect viruses?"

"We're experts with combating viruses and applying antibodies, finding out who did it and why. People can very cleverly and anonymously ruin important stacks of files. There are laws, and the authorities are beginning to use the laws to punish such people."

"Like rustling cattle or siphoning oil."

"Exactly." She hesitated before inquiring, "Siphoning oil?"

"Drilling next to a working oil well and slanting the hole to take from the other well. Like putting a soda straw into someone else's soda."

"People do that?"

"Since they first struck oil." He paused and asked, "In your work with computer viruses do you apply the antibody?"

"No, I don't. That takes another expert. I can find out if it's the operator or the software or if the computer has developed a glitch. I can find out if their terminals are infected by a main computer, which is on all the time. A virus can be stored in the time-and-date system, set to go off at a specific time of a specific day. And I can find out if their programs have been sabotaged. I can narrow it as to why they are losing things. Some people are careless. Or they just made a mistake.''

She then explained, ''One thing about those who plant viruses, there is no danger. It's not a violent crime. It's not cops and robbers at all. The virus-spreaders are either odd jokesters or vengeful fired employees and—''

''No...danger?''

''None at all.'' She was positive. ''But it's always an inconvenience. Umm. This omelet is delicious.''

''I tested it on the cat.''

''Did I get what he left?'' she inquired.

''Now how did you know he was a him?''

''Only a male could look that ratty.''

''You offend me.''

She could have bitten her tongue. She'd forgotten he was a shy scoutmaster from the West Texas oil fields. He probably didn't know much about women. ''I didn't say you looked ratty.''

Her quick glance then surveyed him in an approving manner that made him aware that he was a young male animal, and she was a delectable female of the same species. He shifted on the board bench that served as their chairs, and he swallowed. ''Yes.''

Since that didn't make any sense at all, she looked at him more cautiously.

''I feel ratty,'' he told her. ''That's why I defended the cat.''

"You?"

"I defend all underdo—cats."

"Why would you feel ratty?"

"I'm a house slave."

"Are you really?" She looked at him. "Do you mean you don't have any outside activities? You just plan to run this bed-and-breakfast?"

He'd teasingly meant he was a slave to the Smith renovation, and he'd forgotten the fake bed-and-breakfast was supposed to be his operation. "I have every nickel in this place." That was true. He'd told Nick to wait and pay him when it was finished.

"Well, we'll just have to find a way for you to have a night off before your other guests arrive. You've done a beautiful job of refurbishing this place. It will look as it did when it was built. Why did you put gauze on the walls?"

"That's the way it was done in the olden days. Not plaster, but gauze under the paper. That way, the walls could breathe and the house was cooler."

"How authentic," she stated with contrived seriousness, then she frowned. "You don't plan to air-condition it?"

"No. Air-conditioning is un-Texan. We'll have window screens and fans."

"I'll want to come back when it's all done to look at it." She blotted her lips. "Breakfast was delicious. Thank you."

The fact that she could be curious about his place almost paralyzed his tongue, but he did manage a growly husky reply, "It's just part of the service, ma'am. And Linda, count on supper here. It's a welcome relief for me to sit down to a meal and have someone to talk to." He deliberately hesitated before he added, "I've been very lonely here in Waco."

If he'd hammed it up, she would have scoffed; but he spoke in soft sincerity as he looked down at his plate. He got to her. "Why, yes. I would be delighted. Thank you. But you must let me pay for my own meals. Promise me that."

"You'll pay," he said with such bland certainty.

"I need to rent a car while I'm here. Do you happen to know of a good place?"

"I'd let you have mine, but I do need—"

"Oh, I couldn't let you do that. I'm not at all sure that I could control that car. It seems to me that it leaps around on its own."

"I hadn't thought of it that way. I thought I might be a little careless, but I agree the car does take control. You're right. That's why my thighs and wrists are tired. It's like controlling a cantankerous horse."

She looked at him to see if he was teasing, but she couldn't tell because his eyelashes covered his eyes as he put his fork into the last of his omelet.

"If I may use your phone, I'll call an agency. I believe they deliver the car?"

"I'll take you there. It's on my way."

"Your way. . . to where?"

"To get you to work. It's part of the package."

"I really didn't expect you to be so accommodating. I can't tell you how kind I believe you are. Thank you, yet again."

He smiled like the complacent, ratty cat's calculating big brother.

The car she rented was discreet in style, but it was painted a flashy yellow. He thought it suited her. She was demure but she did have a streak of adventure, just as long as it didn't include mice or dark, rainy nights. What other woman would have stayed in an empty house with a strange man? Of course the Smiths had been there when she'd arrived, and they did look normal and accountable. Hell. So *that* was why she'd stayed. She thought *he* was normal and accountable. Damn.

His car led hers to Stewart's Hardware and Supply, and he left her with a horn toot, which she returned.

Again feeling a tiny flicker of caution, as if there was some danger, he looked around but nothing threatened. Still uneasy, and watching the traffic with more than his usual care, he drove away wondering how she'd get along. She would come home tired tonight, and he'd plan a good meal for her.

It was thinking of *her* that gave him that feeling of danger. He felt there was danger to her? How? There could be none. She was only teaching the Stewart personnel how to use a computer system, after typewriters. Dragging them into the twenty-first century.

But the creepy feeling was similar to what he'd felt when, against all odds, an oil rig had spooked him. He'd learned to pay attention. What was he to do in a situation like this?

Well, tonight he would give her a relaxing bottle of wine so that she would talk to him and tell him about the people who worked in that place.

As he drove back to the Smith house, he thought about Linda whom he'd met just the evening before. How could he become so involved, so taken with a woman in such a short time? It was very strange. But it had been nice having her in the house. He went back to his sham bed-and-breakfast. Inside, waiting for him, was one real owner of the house—Lee Smith.

Three

Mitch saw there were packages at the bottom of the stairs, and he found Lee wandering around looking at the empty rooms. Mitch said, "Well, hi, little mother, how you doing this morning? I didn't see your car in the drive. Getting so you can't get behind the wheel?"

Lee burst into tears.

Mitch was appalled and didn't know what to do. "Lee, for God's sake, what's the matter? Are you in labor? What are you doing here?"

With gaspy, jumping breaths, she snarled, "I still have three weeks to go! You beast!"

"What'd I do?"

"Nothing," she blubbered.

That confused Mitch even more, and he felt a little frazzled. "Lee, what's going on?"

Sniffling into a tissue, making gulping sounds, she managed, "I'm just being pregnant. Don't worry about it. This morning, Nick looked at the Bulge and said, 'Poor tummy.' and I've been weepy ever since.''

"I don't understand."

She wept. "Neither do I."

"Aw, poor baby." He took her into his arms in a tender, very friendly way. "Tell Uncle Mitch all about it."

She warned with great irony, "I can't have a mad, passionate affair with you right now."

"Good thing. Nick's *mean* when it comes to you."

"Is he really?" Lee looked up with a blotched face and red nose and eyes.

"Lee, you have to know that when he said, 'Poor tummy,' he only meant that he wished you didn't have to be uncomfortable. You know how much he loves you. He didn't mind getting you pregnant, but he feels like the whole shebang is out of his control. He really worries that you hurt and there's nothing he can do."

"Really?"

"Really. Women scare the daylights out of men."

"Why?"

"They are so magical. So different. Really precious. Think what it's like for Nick. He loves you, and he got you into this. He's scared for you. He's probably crying today, too. Only he has to go to work, so it'll just eat into his stomach all day and he'll be miserable. Poor guy. He didn't know what to do with you, so he's dumped you off on me—a helpless, hapless bachelor—and he's gotten away."

Lee pulled away and blew her nose. "You were going along real nice, so what turned you so vicious?"

"That's inbred defense. I'm not the kid's daddy, so I'm an innocent bystander. I've given you my quota of sympathy for today. Now you have to wing it on your own." He grinned at her.

"Do you really think Nick worries?"

"He loves you."

Lee gave a trembly sniffle. "All he has to do is hold me and tell me everything will be all right."

"How can he know that?"

"He doesn't have to know it," Lee said the obvious. "All he has to do is *say* it."

"Tell him that," Mitch directed.

"Then I won't believe it."

"Women are baffling."

"So are men."

"Today I'm going to wallpaper the front bedroom for her."

"'For her.'" Lee echoed. "My house, and you're wallpapering the room 'for her.'"

"Yeah," he sighed. "Man alive, I must have been in the boonies too long. She's flipped me."

"Did you sleep with her last night?" Lee questioned indignantly.

Mitch laughed softly. "Thank you. I've never been so flattered. You must think I'm a bear cat of a man."

"I have thought that you were shy."

"Oh, I am," he vowed.

Lee had become doubtful. "You behave yourself with Linda."

"She's old enough, and just because you're pregnant you don't have to be so damned maternal."

Lee put one hand on the Bulge and looked down at it. "Is that what's doing it? I almost came back over here last night."

"I used some of your new bed sheets for Linda's bed."

Lee gasped, "Urrgh! You *undid* those ribbons?"

He appeared somewhat surprised. "Did you mean to just leave the cupboard like that and use *other* sheets?"

"How else?"

"Women are strange."

"We are logical. I am so logical that I have brought the curtains and drapes for the front bedroom."

Mitch smiled. He beamed at her. "What a brilliant woman you are. I'll put them up as soon as I finish the wallpaper."

"And the bedspread. Plus the rugs. Nick brought them in. They're with the drapes at the bottom of the stairs."

"You two are the smartest people I've run into in a barrel of days. So's Linda. Do you know she's a computer expert? Today she's over at Stewart's Hardware and Supply, teaching them how to work a computer system." With just the name of the place, that unsettling feeling returned to Mitch. He tilted his head as he looked at Lee. "You're a native of these here parts, do you know the people at the store?"

"I know Bob Stewart, he's a good man. I know a lot of the people who work there. If I don't know them, I know their families. Anyone who lives for several generations in a town this size, knows those whose families have also lived here that long. There are a couple of people with Bob who are new in town. I've only met them. They seem nice enough. Why? Are you looking for wolves prowling after little Linda June?"

"Is her middle name June?"

"Don't be dense—I was being funny."

"Oh," he said soberly. "What are the new people at the company like?"

"Like I said, nice."

"Nice is like a candy-coated pill."

"Or after-shave to cover up stale sweat."

Mitch laughed. "I've known men like that. They slap on after-shave and feel as if they're shaved and bathed. All they do is stink. Have we any stinkers at Stewart's?"

"Not that I know. Are you getting a little protective of Linda? What could possibly happen to her in that busy place?"

"The back of my neck prickles."

Lee frowned at him. Slowly she said, "I honestly believe there's no danger for Linda at Stewart's."

He stood watching his friend's wife, then told her, "The prickles are still there."

"I'll be darned. You know Nick says that you've got such an instinct for trouble that you spook everybody." She waited a minute, then hesitantly she asked, "What do you think about my baby? Do you think he's okay?"

"Fine." He said it sincerely. Then he took two measured steps to her, lifted his arms like a wooden soldier, patted the top of her head and said in a monotone, "Everything is all right."

"There are times when I don't really even like you."

"Well, you saw Nick first and that probably blinded you."

"I feel I should warn Linda about you."

He shook his head. "That wouldn't be fair. Nobody warned me about her."

"Where did you get that cat?"

"You know, I have the feeling that cat was the primary subject all along, and you have been babbling about all the rest to distract me, and now you feel it's time to hit me with the cat."

"You're safe. I can't bend over to pick up the cat, or I would hit you with it. *When you leave here, that cat goes with you. Understand?*"

He shook his head with slow sadness. "And I thought you were maternal."

"I'm not that type of cat. I mean it. That cat belongs to you."

"He was drawn to the house. He has adopted the house. He's yours."

She enunciated carefully, "Do not upset me. I am pregnant."

"No! Is that right? When're you due?"

"Find a hammer and hand it to me."

"I'm no fool. I must say that although I find you a stimulating conversationalist, I have work to do. Sit by the fire and discourage the cat from staying, while I paper the bedroom. Then you can direct me in hanging the curtains and all. Can you make the stairs?"

"I'm only pregnant, I'm not disabled."

"I could get in back of you and push."

"While you're hanging the paper, I'll think on a reply to that."

Over on the other side of town, at Stewart's Hardware and Supply, Linda had shed her raincoat and met all the people she needed to know. The office section of the company was rather dull but utilitarian. The two top men had private offices that had waist-high glass partitions between them and the other desks. Sitting down, they could see what everyone was doing.

That sounded like management might be harsh taskmasters, but from what Linda had seen the people appeared easy enough. Why should she feel that all was not well? She watched as the employees stopped to exchange talk and smiles. It seemed to be a nice place to work.

Bob Stewart said, "We're sure glad you came down to Waco to help us get started."

"Thank you," Linda replied. She looked through the glass partition at Helen, who was an older employee in that young business. It was Helen who had initiated the computer setup, while Bob had been reluctant. Bob had said that Helen was a whizbang at math, at organization, that she was the real head of the whole operation.

The stray thought came unbidden to Linda that being a whizbang was what it took to put in a virus. Linda discarded such a notion, knowing her conversation with Mitch had planted the stray idea. But there was a strange feeling that something wasn't... quite... right.

The door into the second office opened, and Bob told the new arrival, "Hi, Jim, this is our expert from the computer company, Linda Parsons? Linda, this is my right-hand man, Jim Otter, who hates water. Think of that. An otter who hates water."

Linda offered her hand. "I would bet you've heard that a time or two. Are you a secret swimmer?"

Brusquely dismissive, Jim replied, "I have a water phobia."

Linda managed not to either sympathize or recommend therapy.

Bob was saying, "Jim's just back from a cruise. Can you believe that? A man who hates water—"

"It was a singles cruise on a very large ship." Jim was almost rude in his interruption. Then he seemed to deliberately relax and almost teased Bob, "You're just jealous that you didn't get to go." He lowered his glance to Linda and explained, "Bob's newly divorced and couldn't get things organized in time to go along. He's been here all alone for a month, gnashing his teeth in frustration."

Linda wondered if there was also a professional competition between the two. Who had caused the divorce? Both men were attractive, Jim was a bit older than Mitch. "What do you do here, Jim?"

"Sales."

Short and sweet. He wasn't "selling" Linda. He was too abrupt.

But Jim continued, "Good luck on getting the new program implemented. Bob's a foot-dragger; we need to get into computers."

Bob added, "We lost our payroll, inventory and billings on a mistake. Papers were shredded instead of filed. The computer should solve that. The delay in the payroll, especially, was why I agreed to the expense of the computer and the terminals."

Linda soothed, "After the initial cost, you'll find you save money. And a great deal of time. Everyone will get more done, more efficiently."

Jim assured Linda, "Helen will help you."

Bob then said, "We're all ready. Your people have done it all very well. We put the terminals in the main office for now, so that we can learn the initial part together. Got everything? This side desk can be your home base. You can put your purse in the bottom drawer. There's coffee out at the snack counter. See? Right through that hall. The ladies' room is on down that corridor. Okay?"

"Yes. Thank you." She leaned over, put her purse into the drawer and straightened, conscious of tension between the two men. "Shall we begin?"

It always took a while for the uninitiated to understand they are in control of the computers, Linda knew that. And she knew that they should realize they were already familiar with computers, mankind's sophisticated servants.

Linda told her listeners, "Welcome to the twenty-first century. We now take for granted miracles that didn't exist even five years ago. You've watched your car being tested. You have had physicals. You use coin machines, telephones, you do banking.

"Now you will see what those other people have been using and turn it into a routine that you, too, will take for granted. Learning to use a computer is no different than when you learned to swim, ride a bike or drive a car. It's simple. Just another skill. The magic is in the programming. Just as the wheel made the bicycle possible to ride, this computer allows your mind to fly."

Because her company was truly professional, Linda was so well taught that, in turn, she could teach easily. She made it simple. Which it was.

The morning flew, and lunch was catered. They ate in an excited buzz of exclamations and laughter. And that afternoon, teaching in the specialized sections of how the warehouse people could tap the inventory, or order supplies, or ship it where, made the time disappear.

Anyone who has been on the high of excitement for a sustained period of time, is eventually washed out. At closing time Linda fetched her raincoat, took out her purse, read her map of Waco, smiled goodbyes to the various members of the departing staff, got into her rented car and drove to 1201 Premont...and Mitch.

She was somewhat surprised to realize how excited she was at the thought of seeing Mitch again. She dissected that feeling and decided it was because her room would be changed. Of course. That was why there was such an excited core in her tired body.

Well, he *was* attractive. He moved in a slow, masculine way that was interesting to watch. It was as if he was leashed power. He excited her body. It was strange to feel the fizzling that seeing him caused to go through her network of nerves.

At his house she parked in front along the curb.

The yard was really rather tacky. But it was spring, the bushes and trees were greening and there was a rather rustic charm to the disarray. The bushes needed to be controlled, the tree branches hung too low, and the grass probably hadn't been cut last year at all.

Linda gave a critical glance at the paint-peeling exterior of the house...and saw there were now curtains in "her" windows.

Getting out of the car to stand in the dripping mist, Linda closed the locked car door as she looked around at the other houses. She discreetly stretched her back and moved her shoulders a little. She liked the neighborhood, but it wasn't a commercial area and it seemed an odd place for a bed-and-breakfast. Perhaps that's why Mitch didn't have a sign.

Linda had grown up living in apartments. Her present one in Dallas was on the fifteenth floor, so she found it was very nice to walk up a sidewalk onto a porch. And from the porch she looked around. How...homey.

She heard the front door click and turned toward it.

Mitch opened the door. His glances checking her quickly. "Are you okay?"

"Yes, of course." She became conscious that her muscles were still tensed and she relaxed deliberately.

He asked teasingly, "Forget your key?"

"No. I was just enjoying your porch. It won't be long before you'll have chairs out here for your guests. It will be such a pleasure for traveling people, for those here only for a while."

"It's still a little damp out. Come inside. I have a fire for you and the cat. I think we're going to have to name the ugly thing."

How easily she accepted that she would be a part of the naming. "He's permanent?" And as had happened twenty-four hours before, Linda was lured inside the house by that man.

"I can't just call him 'cat.'"

His voice seemed somewhat husky as she passed him, and he followed her into the house. There he slowly turned to close the door and he locked it.

She felt an odd hesitation as she heard the loud thunk of the dead bolt. She looked back at him, but he was looking at the door.

He had her barricaded inside. She was his. He put his hand flat on the portal with satisfaction, then noted that she was watching him. Uh. There he stood with his hand braced on the door as if to close out all the world. That was the way he felt, but she ought not to know that this soon. Uh. "This door finally fits smoothly," his tongue invented. "It always stuck. It's a pleasure to close it and have it shut so solidly without having to force it." Whew. He ought to start writing fiction. This house was so solidly built that it hadn't shifted one particle of an inch since it had been put up almost a hundred years before. He silently apologized to the long ago genius builder. Mitch told Linda, "This is an old house."

"I like the bare wood floors. You aren't going to put carpeting over these floors, are you?"

"No. Area rugs. A runner on the stairs. Cushions on the window seat on the landing."

"I've never before seen a fireplace in an entrance hall."

He looked back at the other end of the hall to the fireplace there. "It would be welcoming on a blustery winter day when the temperature plummets clear down to thirty degrees."

"Coming inside out of the cold, wouldn't such a fire be a lovely sight."

"With eight bedrooms upstairs, plus the sleeping porch, this house was built for a large family; and they needed places where they could be comfortable without leaving the house. Places they could entertain guests without intruding into the family. So they had this hall, the landing with its window seat, the sitting room at the top of the stairs, the living room and the library. There were places to go."

"Wonderful."

"There's a back stair. It goes up between the storage rooms behind the kitchen at the back of the house and on up to the attic where there were maids' rooms."

"A woman would need help keeping a house this size. Will you have live-in help for your bed-and-breakfast?"

"Not right away. Come see the back stair. You're probably full of kinks from working so hard today, and a little exercise will be good for you."

"It isn't a cold rain. I thought I'd go out in sweats and jog for a mile or so to relax."

"Tough day?"

She just nodded. How could she explain her strange tension at the Stewarts'?

"I'll jog with you. Want to see your room?"

"Did you get the paper on the walls? What color?"

"I sure did, and you'll just have to wait and see. I did a remarkable job of it. Let's go up the back way." He led her through the rooms, and the cat followed through the kitchen and then to the storage rooms.

"Here's the bath I use." He opened a door off the back hall. "This room was the laundry. There were washtubs over here and from this window, clothes were pinned on a line controlled by pulleys. The lines ran outside to a post. See? The washer and dryer are in here, but the outside pulley will be available. Sheets dried in the wind smell good."

"You've thought of everything."

Mitch knew Lee had. He told Linda, "This pantry was used for staples: flour, sugar, home canning, fruits in season and dried fruits. All the trees in the yard were bearing trees, pecan trees, too. This room held large canning pots, and great bowls and platters for entertaining, extra china, linens. See the cupboards? The drawers. The family entertained a lot. With all the lower rooms having double doors that slide back into the walls, they could have a great circulation pattern for guests. Dancing." He had impulsively added that.

They smiled at each other, thinking about the time when the house had been new. Linda said with some melancholy, "People don't entertain in that way anymore."

"In this house—" He caught himself. He was again forgetting it wasn't his house. "—or a house like it, there would be nothing to stop... someone from entertaining just that way."

He—and the cat—showed her how one could make the circle through the storage rooms without ever going into the hall.

"Why did they do that?"

"Winter hide-and-seek?"

"Clever. Clever. I wish I could have known those people. They must have been very special."

They went up the stairs. The cat bounded up ahead of them, then sat at the top and waited for them. It was apparent that the cat had already learned the house.

The stair treads had been sanded and would be refurbished just as had the front stairs. Here too, care had been taken to make the stairwell attractive. It wasn't as wide but a little steeper than the main stair, and it was pretty. Pretty was the right word, Linda thought. There were decorated wood buffers at the corners to protect the walls; but they weren't just buffers, they were cleverly done and quite charming.

Mitch showed Linda through the rest of the rooms and the attic, how the rooms could be accessed through extra doors or a window into a hallway, and at one place through a closet. In his room was a sleeping bag. It was neatly straightened, and the room was very tidy.

He said to her, "Can you find your way now?"

"Perfectly. Thank you for the tour."

"I have to show you your room. You might not look at everything."

"Oh, yes."

He led the way. He even entered her room first and turned to watch her reaction.

She smiled at him a little indulgently, a bit amused, then she looked beyond him and her lips parted in delight.

The room was like summer. The walls were papered in old-fashioned ribbon paper. The drapes were golden and the curtains were sheer and white. The bedspread was a wildly rich pattern enlargement of one segment of the wallpaper. And the rugs were a deep green. It was well done.

"You really bent yourself to do all this today. Thank you."

"It wasn't that hard."

"Anyone who stays here is going to love this room."

"It should have been blue." His voice was soft and husky as he looked soberly into her blue eyes.

She tore her gaze away from his and eventually focused her eyes, looking around the room with great pleasure. Then she glanced at her watch. With credible efficiency she declared, "You have ten minutes if you expect to jog with me."

In a sassy, very masculine tit-for-tat way, he replied, "I only need two."

She snatched up her purple jogging suit and ran from the room, her heels ringing on the bare floors.

Four and a half minutes later when she erupted from the bath he was leaning against the opposite wall with his arms crossed on his wide chest. She stopped dead in her tracks and laughed. Then she went into her room and put on her pink socks and white running shoes.

The rain was only a thick mist. They ran squishily through the neighborhood getting damper with every stride. Their eyelashes were wet. Their hoods, shoulders, thighs and forearms were soggy, their spirits climbed. Exuberant, they got back to the sham bed-and-breakfast to find the cat on the front porch, just far enough back to stay dry as it waited for them.

Linda asked, "Did you let him out?"

In disgust Mitch replied, "Endlessly. While my momma didn't raise her baby to be no cowboy, she didn't raise him to be a cat doorman, either. That cat is so territorial that it makes you wonder who's in charge. Instead of being a hobo, wandering on his own, he's more than likely an overthrown dictator."

Linda laughed, very amused.

They parted to change into dry clothes. Linda quickly rinsed off in the cold shower, put on a lounging suit of soft blue that made her blue eyes even bluer. She surveyed herself in the bathroom mirror, added a little dark blue eyeshadow and a touch of dark mascara, and she was ready.

She went down the back stairs, into the back hall and then into the kitchen. He turned his head quickly, surprised to see her coming from a different direction; but he smiled, looked down her and back up to her eyes. Then he said, "Your supper is served." And he handed her a glass of wine.

She was carrying her wet jogging suit. "Where did you put yours? May I put mine in the dryer?"

"I was waiting for yours. Let me take it." And he put them in the dryer and started the machine knowing their suits would intermingle.

She should have expected that supper, exactly. What does any man think of when he thinks of a "good meal"? Steak, baked potato, salad and apple pie.

She asked that her steak be cooked longer, and he
was appalled. She retorted that she'd seen steers hurt
worse than that get well!

He groaned at the ancient raw-beef joke. "Now,
how did a city woman from Dallas ever hear that old
expression?"

She explained the obvious, "We're close by Fort
Worth. We read their paper on occasion. We've become more civilized while Fort Worth is stuck in an
1870's time warp. Mostly deliberately. They milk it."

"How can you milk a steer?"

She had to put her hand to her forehead and groan
softly, as if he wasn't to know that she groaned, then
she replied with exaggerated patience, "They milk the
1870's."

And he laughed at her in great delight. He would
marry her. Yes, he would. She was a treasure.

They sat at the contrived table, on the ladder-
supported bench, and ate the pie, which naturally had
vanilla ice cream on top of it.

The Smiths came by. Linda thought they must be
very good friends, indeed, who not only visited every
night but walked inside without knocking.

"Come in, come in," Mitch welcomed in great good
humor as if the three shared a joke of some sort.
"Want some pie?"

Mrs. Smith said, "That cat's still here."

Mitch told Linda, "Lee doesn't like cats."

"Lee?" Linda smiled at Mrs. Smith. "My name's
Linda. I met you yesterday."

"I remember." Lee wasn't quite sure what to do
then. Nick was there to see the almost finished bedroom.

But Nick handled it. "How'd the wallpaper go up-stairs?"

"Real easy. Go up and see. Do you mind, Linda?"

He considered it her room. "No. Not at all."

Mitch said to the Smiths, "You guys go on up and snoop around. We'll finish up here."

Given permission in their own house, and with the cat running ahead, Lee and Nick went out the double doors into the living room and then on beyond into the hall and disappeared.

"Good friends?" Linda inquired.

"The best." Mitch nodded in satisfaction, knowing they were.

But his smile was one of humor. Linda wondered why Mitch seemed so amused. It had to be a friend joke of some sort. That was like family jokes. They must be very close to have acquired that sort of relationship. Linda was a touch envious. Her friends were scattering, marrying or changing jobs and moving away from Dallas, or becoming involved with other people, other circles of acquaintances.

She looked at Mitch who was eating the rest of another piece of ice-cream-topped pie. She thought he would keep his friends. He would call them occasionally or send a clipping that interested them or write postcards. He would keep in touch. "Did you make the pie?"

"No. See how honest I am with you?" He wondered if she realized what he was telling her. He went on, "There's a bakery here in Waco that doesn't import frozen dough and call it homemade bread, and they don't import frozen pies, done dozens at a time. They make all their own. They even have a crumbled-cookie jar, and there are days when something isn't sold because a batch didn't come out to please them."

"I want to see that place. Tell me the address. Do they do those marvelously scandalous squishy doughnuts?"

"How could you know?"

"I strongly suspect that you're a hedonist. The first clue is homemade bread and homemade pies. That's the beginning. Then you eat with concentration. You relish the food. Last night's frozen foods were not the bin type, either. Do you have them made up?"

"Now, how did you know?"

"I'm familiar with all the frozen fast foods available in the marketplace. Those last night weren't like any that I've ever had. They weren't packaged, they were simply foil-wrapped. Do you make up your own?"

"No." His smile only crinkled the sides of his eyes. Smugly he told her, "I have a source."

If she'd had a sword, she would have put the point to his throat. "Give me the name."

With the confidence of a man who is on the inside, he said, "They have all the customers they want. They don't want to expand."

"How nasty of them."

He laughed. Then he lifted his brows as he lowered his eyelids just about halfway in the most confident male side-glance imaginable, and he tempted, "I can get all I want."

"Doughnuts for ninety-five Stewart people for tomorrow morning?"

In his best Mafia manner and accent, he put his paper-towel napkin on the table and said, "Gotta make a call." Then he paused and asked, "Wot's it worth ta ya?"

"Ah-ha! You're inviting bribery."

"Yeah. Sure." He smiled slightly, and put his arms out while he shrugged once.

Did he know how beautifully that showed off his body? Linda looked down him in pleasure. He was so hard, so male, very male. Yes.

"I'll think of a way you can be grateful."

Cautioning, Linda began to demur, "Uhh..."

And the Smiths returned from upstairs, followed by a herding cat.

Four

Mitch straddled their contrived bench and said to Lee, "If you get into the living room before I do, you can have the chair. Or you can clear the table and do the dishes." He was telling her to sit down and relax.

She went into the living room, escorted by the cat.

Nick stood around in their way, as Mitch and Linda cleared away the dishes and tidied the kitchen. Then the three went into the living room with Lee, who said, "This cat has been treating me like a guest. He sits there, alert, watching me and appears to expect me to make conversation."

"Did you? Were you courteous?" Mitch inquired.

Lee killed Mitch with a glance.

In her blue lounging suit, Linda sat cross-legged on the floor, and the two men settled down nearby. Nick wrapped one hand around Lee's ankle and then began to question Mitch on what he'd done and what was still to be done.

Linda thought how amazing it was for Nick to be that curious about Mitch's house. Nick seemed genuinely interested. He appeared a little nosy, asking prices and things that were none of his business, but Mitch didn't take offense. Lee cleared her throat admonishingly a couple of times, so it was obvious even she thought that Nick was beyond the bounds of propriety.

It really wasn't very long before the Smiths rose to their feet and prepared to leave. Until then, Linda hadn't realized she'd thought they were intrusive. Now, why would she think Mitch's friends had been there too long? Well, she wanted him to herself. How strange. She looked at Mitch, standing there with his hands in his jeans pockets, smiling at his friends, waiting for them to leave.

They did leave.

Downstairs all the inside doors were hung on tracks and could be rolled back into the walls. Looking through the library from where she sat in the living room, Linda watched as Mitch closed the front door after the Smiths with that same solid clunk. Again he put his big hand flat on the panel in marked satisfaction.

That door must have annoyed him, for him to be so pleased it would close properly. Then he turned his head and looked at her.

His look made her insides shiver. He looked like a lion standing just beyond a campfire. It had to be the small flames in the fireplace that made his green eyes look that way.

If he'd licked his lips and bared his teeth at her, she wouldn't have been surprised. But he blinked and smiled just a little, and she was surprised to see that he was only the shy scoutmaster. Where had the lion gone? Had it even been there? Why did she feel that flicker of disappointment?

Then across the hall and through the library he prowled toward her, and the quiverings inside her began again. He watched her as he came clear across that endless library into the living room. He never took his eyes from her, and she knew that because she watched him every step of the way.

She couldn't breathe. She could hardly blink and the one time she did, she had trouble getting her eyelids back open. There were little tremors in her body as if she was chilled, and her teeth pretended they wanted to chatter, although her skin surface was too hot—from being so close to the fireplace, of course.

He squatted down next to her and reached . . . past her to the transistor radio that sat on the hearth. He turned it on, concentrating on it. He was much too close to her. She was struggling to act like a normal adult, while he hovered over her like a beast of prey. And that excited her body in a really amazing way.

He found a station that was playing loud, raucous, foot-stomping music, which jolted her rather rudely. But it was just the wildness she needed to spend the restlessness that had caused such a turmoil inside her. He stood up, held a hand down to her and in a very husky voice suggested, "Let's try out the floors for dancing."

It was fun! He strutted and showed off, and she threw her arms around and moved her body and was outrageous. She'd never in her whole life been so knowingly provocative. She sashayed and pranced and flirted. He stomped and moved, *gorgeously* male, like a woods creature luring a female in a mating dance.

At the commercial break, they stopped and stood facing each other, separated by perhaps three feet, and they laughed. Breathless, stimulated, they laughed to share that attracted stimulation.

Then he changed the station to swelling music that lifted her sensitized insides in tingles. Without a word, he came to her and took her into his arms in the dancing manner. But before he began to move, he pulled her slowly close to him, his solemn gaze on hers; and her body touched his and was held against him.

It was where she had wanted to be. Until then he hadn't really touched her. And she realized that she had longed for it. Now she was against him, and her whole body was enjoying his so that it alarmed some remote segment of her mind. Her body had surrendered to him. She was confused by herself. She didn't…she wanted…she should…why didn't he… Then he moved with the music, and her feet tangled.

She said "Sorry," and blushed.

He paused, tightened the grip of his big hand spread at the small of her back, and bent his head over her like a predator, his eyes intent. He was too close. Her breasts lifted against him, and her back pressed forward. She felt her face become scarlet as her body rubbed a little against him. That faint little conscience of hers was shocked.

Her knees were weakened. To help them and give them more support, she stretched up so that her arm was around his shoulder. And the diminishing conscience was scandalized.

They danced to the music, their bodies each relishing being against the other. Their faces were serious, their eyes focused so closely that they were unaware of anything else in the room, of anything beyond the close range of invisible barrier that enclosed them.

Linda felt just a little odd, faint, boneless, breathless. She wasn't sure of anything except that if he carried her upstairs to his sleeping bag she would be helpless to protest. The objecting conscience had vanished. She was a wanton?

Her languid eyes went to their clasped hands. His swallowed hers. His was strong and sun-browned. Struggling with heavy lids, she looked up at his face above hers. His stare was so intent, she could see the flames in his irises even though his back was to the fireplace. He was so serious that the little sun crinkles at the corners of his eyes showed pale against his tan.

He was after her.

In her mind the conscience had returned. He *was* after her.

She swallowed awkwardly and said, "You're a very good dancer." To dance well was strange for a shy scoutmaster from the wilds of West Texas.

He kissed her forehead, a soft salute from firm lips. But Linda felt the thrill of it puff her lips before it slid down into her body. There the sensation separated to touch the insides of her nipples before it flowed down to lick along her stomach. She gasped as the feeling slithered along the insides of her thighs in a sweep, before it concentrated in a pulsing swirl at the core of her.

She looked so big-eyed, he wondered if he'd offended her, but she didn't move away. Then his head just went down, and his lips found hers waiting. He took a harsh breath through his nose in surprise at her soft mouth opening to his. His arms tightened and his stance faltered, but his feet corrected that. He braced himself and found she was almost limply holding onto him.

Breathing in a pant, he lifted his mouth from hers and his eyes gleamed as he smiled. She, too, panted. Her breasts were pushed against him with every breath, and her body was malleable. With firm discipline, he kept his hands from moving, but by hugging her and shifting his arms a little he moved her body against his very sneakily.

He groaned as if in great agony. Then he buried his face into that dark mass of hair that clung to him like silk, and he deliberately breathed into her ear to cause goosebumps to riot over her surface and tickle her in secret places. He wanted her. What if he went ahead and told that to her? She might just as well know. What would she do if he just baldly told her that? She might even say okay. She might feel just exactly as he did and want him just as much. So he said, "I want you." He watched as she blinked, but she didn't get indignant. She was deciding. She'd say yes. Watch, she *would* say yes.

"No."

It was such an automatic, rather unorganized and confused word, that he laughed in a soft, throaty way that made her condition much worse. Unfairly he suggested, "I revolt you."

She dragged up the heavy lids and looked at him fuzzily. Moving her lips in what an unprejudiced bystander would label invitingly, she replied "no" more firmly than the first time. Then her mind struggled to be coherent as she communicated: "I don't believe you're as shy as your friends think."

That made him laugh in gusts, trying not to but being unable not to laugh.

She blinked at the sound of that laugh. "How did you make them think you were shy?"

"Who told you that?"

"Lee said it that first night. When they left."

"I am a little shy."

"You don't kiss shy."

"How do you know?"

She let go of his shoulder with one hand, secure in the knowledge that he would hold her upright, and she gestured while she said, "I've seen X-rated films."

"Why, Linda Parsons! You shock me."

"Your kiss shocked me."

"I was just being friendly."

Ineffectively, as if she wasn't at all serious about it, she moved to get free, and he did loosen his arms somewhat. That annoyed her and she frowned at him. "That was not a friendly kiss." She meant to say only that, but her busy mouth went on: "That's a preliminary one."

"Oh?" asked the shy one. "Preliminary to... what?" And he contrived to look innocently curious.

No innocent man could look that innocent. She groused, "You've set up this bed-and-breakfast in order to lure unsuspecting female flies into your spider web."

But she didn't move away from him. She was just lying in his arms, arguing about whether or not he was trying to seduce her.

She saw that he was amused. His untanned crinkles had disappeared in the creases of his humor. He would make a poor liar. The crinkles would betray him. "One thing about you," she told him out of left field. "You could never lie."

That jolted Mitch. He'd already lied to her. Why had she said that now? "Why do you say that?"

"You'd be too amused with your lie to do it properly."

"I hadn't realized there was a proper way to lie. Teach me to lie properly."

"You already know how to do that. You said you wanted me, when you know full well that you don't know me well enough to do something... To do... To..."

"To do what?"

"Something that... intimate."

He had a very great inner struggle not to laugh. She was precious. Her eyes were serious as she lay there in his arms. She was earnest, watching him as if she wanted him to deny that he didn't know her well enough to make love to her. So she was tempted! Hot dog. She was interested. She was toying with getting him to argue her into doing it. Knowing she could always pull back and be indignant, she wanted to be tempted a little bit more. She wanted to experiment in playing with fire.

On fire, he was willing. The quicker he could get her used to him, the quicker he could get her. He kissed her again. That almost blew the stack. He lifted his mouth from hers, and he chuffed and blew and shivered like a bull on the other side of a strong, high fence from an alluring and probably receptive cow.

She was no cow.

She raised her unusually heavy lashes. His face was quite close and she had trouble focusing. His eyes were getting bloodshot, and she could feel him tremble. She shifted to relieve him of her weight, but he clutched her to him. And he kissed her yet again.

Her head spun. It would have been interesting to have stood aside and seen that, for if hers spun around that way, his head would have had to follow hers because his mouth was firmly feasting on hers, really quite greedily.

It was remarkable to experience her body's response to just being held and accepting kisses. No wonder people kissed. She'd always thought it was a pleasant thing to do, but she'd never had anything like the kisses given to her, taken from her by Mitchell Roads.

More interesting, she had never been aware of all the roots that led from her mouth to all sorts of places in her body. His kisses were root stimulators. And her roots were alive and well, writhing in quite scandalous, sinuously erotic delight. She liked it.

But what one likes and what one is permitted to do are often at variance with one another. According to the rules, she was supposed to behave properly. So with some effort Linda puffed her lips to speak, but Mitch took that as another invitation. He puffed his own lips to meet hers, then he brought the tip of his tongue into play, and Linda found her mouth involved in a duel that was shockingly pleasurable.

Discipline struggled to surface, to take control, and she made sounds. His supporting hand allowed her to pull her head back a tad, and she managed to mumble "Twenty-seven hours."

His eyes glittered. "Tomorrow?"

With great effort, she formed the denying words: "Since yesterday." She was trying to tell him she hadn't known him long enough to be so intricately wound around him this way.

He drew in a breath to argue, and the doorbell chimed. With no drapes in the house and with all the double doors slid back into the walls, they were completely visible from the porch. Who would dare interrupt? What brainless, heartless idiot would snatch this beginning opportunity from him? He really didn't care to find out.

But the doorbell insisted.

He reluctantly released a nicely malleable, unresisting woman and left her standing there by the fireplace, her two hands holding her head level so that she could stand up.

His face not at all welcoming, he opened the door and snapped, "Yes, Molly? What do you want?"

"Well, sugar, I didn't think you were ever going to answer the door, and I have this nice pie I promised you this morning. I know you like your sweets hot." And before he could slam the door, she'd placed the hot pie in his hands and slid past him into the entrance hall.

There, the newcomer's hostile stare raked the rather rumpled Linda Parsons with great distaste. Her sugary voice exclaimed falsely, "Oh, I didn't know you had company."

It might well have been a hot potato he was juggling and not a pie made of Molly's usual glue and unknowns. If Linda said one thing about being a bed-and-breakfast guest, everything would hit the fan. "Sorry, Molly, but we're past due for an appointment. You will excuse us." He made it a statement.

"Where're you going?" Her eyes were on a gradually recovering Linda. "You didn't say anything this morning about going out tonight."

"We have so many desserts from the store, that perhaps you'd like to give this pie to another of your neighbors?" He tried to hand it back.

"I made it just for *you*!" Molly had a practiced pout.

"I can't eat it all. Thanks anyway. See you around." He put the pie back in her hands in a way that she either had to take it or spill it down her front.

If she'd let it spill, then he'd have had to let her clean it off her chest; but she'd just heated the pie and it would still be hot, maybe too hot. She'd been checked.

Linda stared at the interchange between Molly and Mitch. Mitch and Molly? Had he been fooling around with this Molly? Why else was she bringing him pies?

Mitch looked at his watch. "You understand." He took Molly's arm and was firm about getting her back to the still open door.

But Molly wasn't that maneuverable. "Who is she?"

"My guest. Watch the door." He eased her through quite firmly and said a flat, "Good night." Then he closed and locked the door.

He looked at Linda, still standing where he'd left her. She was slowly coming out of her sexual daze. Damn. He smiled and asked, "Where were we?"

Linda asked, "Was the pie that you gave—"

"Are you kidding? I wouldn't do that to you. She makes them out of glue and whatever."

"Then you accepted a pie?" Linda asked.

"I thought I was being polite to the Smi—to a neighbor. But I could hardly get her out of the house. I did try that first pie. I don't think I really want to know what was in it. It might have been something nasty."

"She makes you pies? Plural? More than this one?"

"She forces pies on me. I even told her I was on a diet. Nothing works. She just pops up with another. I pitch them. She's a damned nuisance."

"That's rude."

"So's Molly."

"Did you kiss her?"

"No. I only kiss women named Linda Parsons."

He came back to her, and her pupils expanded rather remarkably. That gave him courage and he took her back into his arms, but she resisted. "Don't let her bother you," Mitch told Linda. "She'll eventually go home."

"Eventually?" Linda looked through the library windows, which faced onto the porch, and there stood Molly—watching them. "She's out there."

"She's weird."

Linda looked up at Mitch, but she stepped back from him. "She has good taste."

"Not in pies."

"In men," Linda specified.

"You haven't tasted me yet."

"She's still there."

"Let's go out and drive around the block. She'll think we're gone."

"Have you encouraged her?" she inquired.

"No."

"She needs a friend."

"Good Lord, no. There's a limit to what I'll do for any woman. She's out to hook a man, and I'm just handy. She came on to me so strong that first day that she scared the . . . dickens out of me."

Linda smiled. He really was shy. She glanced over at the windows again, but Molly had left.

"There was a man at the office that way."

"Oh?" Mitch became intensely alert. "What did you do?"

"I talked to him about a fake man. I made one up. There was no man who interested me especially there at the office, and anyway office romances aren't a good idea. So every time this guy came around, I talked about how the invisible man was quicker, better, stronger, everything. No man can stand that sort of competition, and he finally wandered off and left me alone."

"Are you going to start telling me about another man?"

"No."

Mitch smiled. "Let's go drive around. I'll treat you to an ice-cream cone."

She replied slowly. "Okay." She knew that she'd just revealed that she was interested in Mitch. And after those steaming-hot kisses she'd allowed him, it wasn't friendship that she was wanting. She had betrayed herself. Now was the time to say something businesslike and go upstairs to her room and end this beginning madness. Now was the time. Now.

He helped her into her raincoat, and pulled on his. She took his offered hand, they went out of the house, down the steps and to his car. They got into it and drove out about the city. Driving gave Mitch something to do with his hands. They finally took the road around Lake Waco as they talked, exchanging information about themselves, and they went for an ice-cream cone in that drizzly, cool evening.

Then he drove her back to the Smiths' house. He helped her up the porch steps and his body was tingling. What if... What if...

But inside the door at the bottom of the stairs, she said, "Thank you for dinner and the ice cream. Good night, Mitch."

He didn't actually believe she was putting him off, but he allowed it. He didn't want to try giving her any unwanted "pies" and being rejected. "Good night."

She allowed Mitch a rather chaste kiss, then she turned away. He would have watched her bottom go up those stairs, but the cat wanted to go outside.

While Mitch was accommodating the cat's wishes, Linda vanished up the stairs.

As she prepared for bed, Linda thought about the evening and about Mitch's kisses. She again felt his arms around her so tightly, with one of his big, hard hands holding her head steady. And she remembered how it felt to be against his strong, excited body. She thrilled to the memory of having him so concentrated on just her. How stiff his hard hands were as they'd moved on her back, petting her, rubbing her, pressing her against him.

She was swamped with sensations shivering through her as she remembered feeling him so strong, hard. Her body was still so sensitive that it throbbed with desire. It shocked her that she felt such excitements.

That brought her conscience to her attention. She hadn't behaved very well. She had felt so marvelously attracted that she'd allowed all the safety rules to slide away while she experienced the rapture.

But . . .

She didn't know Mitch. She'd only met him the night before. He was a charming, shy man. Wasn't he? He handled himself remarkably well for a shy man. But his friends, the Smiths, had said he was shy, and they knew him very well. They were close friends so they would know if he was shy or not, wouldn't they?

She'd allowed Mitch the kind of kisses no man had ever taken from her. She hadn't just allowed it, she'd helped him. His kisses had been delicious, deliriously so. She had read about such kisses, but those she'd experienced hadn't come close to such magic. She'd thought such descriptions were only the writer's imagination. Such kisses were real. And shocking.

She ought to be careful of Mitch. She had no intention of getting involved in a light affair with a man who wasn't even a native of Waco. What if she fell in love with him and he went off, back to West Texas away from Dallas?

A woman didn't get to the age of twenty-seven, intact, without learning to protect herself. If she was smart, she wouldn't conduct a dalliance with the innkeeper. She might flirt a little but she would keep it as a light entertainment, that's what she'd do.

After those kisses? Now how was she going to accept the sipping kisses of a light flirtation when he was capable of kindling all her senses? Could she deny herself a repeat experience of that tempting, living fire, that remarkable ecstasy that licked along her nerves and trembled inside her, making her shiver with desire?

Well, she might allow him just that much and no more. She could stop him.

Yeah? And who was going to stop her?

She had to consider how it might be for Mitch. If he was as shy and inexperienced as, in fact, she was, would it be fair to use him and then to step away? Be a tease?

What she really wanted was to be a siren and tease him until he was out of control. That very night, if the doorbell hadn't rung at that particular time, she might very well have rung Mitch's bell.

She went to sleep thinking about the consequences of doing that. And her dreams were wild and erotic. She awoke all sweaty and needy; she'd clawed the sheets and wondered what she'd begun.

What if she just got up and went down the hall to Mitch's room? Would he have any protection? She didn't. Perhaps she should get some? How did one introduce such a subject to a man who was practically a stranger?

That question alone should have told her just how much off base she was in this madness. She was far ahead of any logical conduct. She needed to settle down, back off and pretend last night's magic hadn't happened. That is what she should do.

Could she? Could she treat Mitch now as the stranger he really was? She would have to try, or she should move out and leave him alone. She really ought not to tamper in someone's life just because she was curious about what would happen if she was reckless and allowed him the freedom of her body.

Damn. She was swamped with regret. Well, better regret now than later. She could really get herself into a peck of trouble just from being curious. She would behave. She would. She'd better.

It was some time before Mitch could settle down and become calm enough to go up the stairs past Linda's door—which was more than likely locked—and go to his own room.

The cat was already there waiting to share his sleeping bag. Mitch said in a very sour way, "It isn't you I want in here. Why don't you scat?"

The cat closed his eyes to contain his humor.

Disgruntled, Mitch peeled out of his clothes and for that night slept his usual way: stark naked. He hoped she had nightmares and came running. He'd be ready.

How had he lived for thirty years and never met anyone like Linda? She was so amazing. Just to look at her was thrilling. It didn't make sense. There were other pretty women. He'd seen his share, why Linda Parsons?

Why couldn't Linda have Molly's eagerness? Molly repelled him. She was as pretty as Linda, why would he reject Molly and not Linda? What was the magic in Linda that made him know she was what he wanted? The only one in all his thirty years to excite him to this positive reaction, this need, this yearning? It was peculiar.

He turned over inside the sleeping bag, and on the outside the cat hissed in temper. Absently Mitch said, "Sorry."

He thought Linda moved so wondrously. Just the fact that he could use the word "wondrously" showed he was in some kind of mind warp. He wasn't in control. She'd mesmerized him. Cast a spell. Voodooed him. He was a victim.

How could she kiss him that way and then leave him alone for the night? That was cruel and inhuman treatment. He ached. He got up, went downstairs to his bathroom and took a shower, standing under the hot water for a long time.

And he realized he hadn't arranged a hot bath for Linda. She'd had to rinse off in the cold water. She'd never said one word. Guilt riding him, he wondered what should he do? Go wake her up and invite her down to his shower and offer to soap her down? He'd do that. He wouldn't mind. He'd soap his hands and... He'd be better off not thinking that way.

Just watch, in the morning she would come down the stairs like nothing had happened. She'd smile and say "Good morning," like he was just another man. And she'd eat a hearty breakfast and trot off to Stewart's Hardware and Supply and not even give him a thought. That's what would happen.

Mitch dried his tender skin, put on fresh underwear and trudged back upstairs to his narrow sleeping bag. He had to push the stubborn cat over so that he could crawl inside. Then he stretched out and put his mind firmly to planning exactly how he'd go about the next day's work.

So he controlled himself. He was pleased that was so. He was the captain of his ship and the master of his soul.

Until he slept.

Five

As he had the day before, Mitch turned off the alarm and was first out of his unfairly limited share of the sleeping bag. He said to the cat, "It's nice you're good for something. I haven't seen a mouse since you arrived, but you could have left a couple. If she'd run into one last night, she would have hightailed it in here and jumped into my sack with me." He pulled on the necessary clothing and went downstairs to start coffee and stare pensively out at the beautiful, sun-filled Texas day.

Before he could pamper Linda by carrying her coffee up to her, he heard her heels tapping down the front stairs. He turned in anticipation of her blinding smile.

She hesitated in the doorway, pale and wan. She said, "Mitch—"

"Are you okay?"

She nodded, avoiding his stare, backing away from the reach of his hands. "Mitch, my conduct was abominable last night. I've never acted that way in all of my adult life, or even in my young life, and I don't know why I behaved so outrageously with you, but I am sorry. I beg your pardon."

And she riveted him. He was the only man she'd kissed or tempted the way she had kissed and tempted *him* last night? He was exuberant! And she was apologizing? The darling woman. She was a treasure. He'd marry her. He cleared his throat so that he wouldn't squeak in excitement and blabber that she drove him crazy, so that he could speak in a normal, adult way: "You're forgiven. I'll probably be warped the rest of my life, but I can understand uncontrolled behavior. Women are like that and—"

"You can—" Her sentence was broken as she gasped in outrage. "You *forgive* me?"

Her eyes shot sparks, and he was fascinated to actually see that. He explained in surprise, "You asked me to."

"I was just being courteous. It was all *your* fault! I wouldn't have acted that way if you'd controlled yourself, you lecher!"

"I—"

She closed her eyes as she put her hands over her ears. "I don't want to hear it! Hush! How can you stand there and act like a victim? Who was holding me up last night, taking advantage of me? You were! You rake! How dare you!" A corner of her mind was appreciating the drama. She especially liked calling him a rake.

"Look, petunia, you came into my life and turned it upside-down. And now you want me to apologize to you about you behaving like a voraciously lusty vampire?" He was enjoying himself immensely. She was susceptible to him! Pretty soon he would allow her to kiss him as she begged him to let her stay.

"I'm packed. It's probably better if I move to a hotel."

"No!"

She gave him a scathing, raking glance, "You'd be safer with me out of your house."

And he laughed.

There are just times that men should not laugh, and apparently this was one of them.

She lost her temper entirely. She drew herself up so that her eyes were level with his chin and she said, "How dare you." She was magnificent.

"Now, honey—"

"I am Miss Parsons!"

"Yes, Miss Parsons, honey. Don't you know that you tilt me? I can't believe that it's you who's my first guest. I think I'll close down this bed-and-breakfast business and steal you away. I'll even marry you. That has to be a miracle, since we don't know each other at all. We can get acquainted as we go along, Miss Parsons. Won't it be awkward for me to be calling you Miss Parsons when the babies start coming along? And anyway, you can't leave or I'll sue you and your company for every dime you all have, for breach of contract." He thought that was hilarious. If he sued, what would they do when they found out he wasn't a bed-and-breakfast owner after all, and he was in a restricted, noncommercial neighborhood and the house wasn't even his?

She paused. Yes, he could create a scandal. How would she ever face her boss, who would look at Linda and simply stare in gentle shock. Linda could not endure that. She said, "I will finish the week."

"I appreciate that. And for supper I'll give you enchiladas again as a peace offering." He smiled as she glanced at him. "Now sit down. I have eggs Benedict for your breakfast. Hunger makes the best of us cranky," he told her blithely. "I believe all tempers are gentled by a full tummy. I would even be glad to rub yours if you think that might help?"

She snubbed him, going into the dining room and sitting stiffly at the contrived table.

He couldn't believe she'd agreed to stay. He served them both as he commented on the sunny day. He mentioned that the cat had cleared out the mice. That got her attention. And he said they still had to name the cat. He'd be glad of any help she could give on that problem.

He sat alongside her as if that was his privilege, and she sneaked little peeks at him. He ate an enormous breakfast. He relished it so much that she quit toying with her food and sampled it, and finished by eating it all.

He gave her another cup of coffee in a companionable way, and he walked with her out onto the porch where there were two great white cartons. He cocked his head at her in a flirting way as he explained, "Your doughnuts."

"You...you got them? Oh, how marvelous! Thank you. I'll give you a check when I get home. Do you need the money now?" She snatched her glance from a lightning peek at his worn jeans.

She'd just called the Smiths' house "home." He liked the sound of it and he replied in easy humor,

"The doughnuts are one of my first-guest prizes. It was in the small print on your registration."

"I can't allow that. You're too kind." But she wondered about his lovemaking. Was that one of the guest prizes, too? Romance the ladies?

Effortlessly, Mitch lifted the big boxes of doughnuts and carried them to her rented car at the front curb.

She hurried along, exclaiming, "Two hundred doughnuts are a lot. Here, put them on the backseat. Thank you very much."

"You're welcome. Enchiladas for supper," he reminded her.

She blushed, paused awkwardly, then rushed around the car and got into it. She put the key into the ignition and looked to be sure he was clear of the car.

She eased away from him and he watched her drive off, but again he felt that weird prickling of danger.

As she drove along, she thought how kind he had been to order the doughnuts. That made it difficult for her to maintain her wrath for an innkeeper who was in her doghouse. Mitch. He hadn't shaved, and she wished he'd whiskered her. Wait a minute, Linda Parsons! She was rejecting exactly that kind of an attitude.

She drove to Stewart's and there she was brisk and businesslike as she opened boxes and offered the deliciously big and squishy glazed doughnuts.

Bob Stewart chewed on one before he said, "I went by your bed-and-breakfast place, but you weren't registered. Do you use another name?"

Not only her eyes but her entire mind blinked. What did he mean, she wasn't registered? Well, she hadn't signed a registry. That had been an oversight. Mitch had probably forgotten. "The phone number was changed. Here, I'll put down the correct one." Then she asked Bob, "Was there some problem?"

"No, not at all. I just thought maybe, being a stranger in town and all, that you might like to get out of your room and have supper in one of our showcases. This is a great town."

"I was busy. I do have acquaintances. Thank you, but you needn't be concerned for me."

"Well, it wasn't just . . . duty. I wanted to see you."

Apparently men were men, even outside Dallas. She was silent and busy, not sure how to reply. She could say: Last night I was involved somewhat with one of my acquaintances. Or she could say: It's just a good thing you weren't on that front porch with Molly becau— Or maybe that would have been the solution to Molly! Bob and Molly. Molly wouldn't have been at all reticent. She'd have pitched that glue pie over into the bushes and grabbed Bob. Linda looked at Bob. Molly didn't deserve him.

Bob said to Linda, "How about supper tonight. It's Friday. We could go out and celebrate making it through another week."

"Sorry. I have a supper date." Frozen enchiladas on a plank table in an empty, gauze-walled room with Mitchell Roads, who had set her whole life off kilter in the first twenty-seven hours.

If she was smart, she'd cancel Mitch and go with Bob. Bob was harmless, while Mitch was the most dangerous thing that had ever come her way. The only danger in her life, besides Mitch, had been a black, silent truck that had almost taken her out on a dark, foggy street. She still had nightmares about the truck.

In the years to come, would she have nightmares of another kind, about a blond, green-eyed innkeeper?

Bob was saying, "—nd Festival is Sunday. How are you with kites?"

The word "kites" was the clue that Bob spoke of Waco's Wind Festival. "My innkeeper is going to take me to that."

"Sam?"

"Oh, no. Mitch."

Bob's glance went aside in scrambling thought, then his interested stare returned to Linda. He smiled and said, "Met a new friend?"

Linda almost frowned. Bob's tone had been somewhat insinuating. *Had* he been on the porch when Mitch had kissed her in that steamy, sinful, scandalous way that had made her knee want to slide up along his thigh while her hands clutched? Molly had walked up on the porch without them hearing her; had Bob been out there, too? No, he didn't say the doorbell went unanswered; he said she wasn't listed as registered. When had he been there?

Linda became *very* businesslike and efficient. "He isn't a 'new friend,' he's just an acquaintance."

Bob thoughtfully watched her blush.

Linda called the Stewart employees to order and asked, "Did you wash all that doughnut goop off your fingers?" And, by George, some got up and went to wash.

The employees, plus Bob and Jim, settled down at their terminals or stood nearby watching, or sat close by on either side of the terminals. When everyone was settled and attentive, Linda asked, "What's the most important thing to do?"

So chorused that they must have practiced, their reply came: "Turn it on."

She laughed nicely, and the rest enjoyed that. "Okay, smarties. As you work, what do you do?"

In a roar, they replied, "Save and copy!"

"And at the end of the day?"

Several scrambled replies said versions of: "Off-site."

"The copies are important. Never go without a backup copy. But taking one copy offsite, to another place, is vital. If there's a fire, or a mistake of any kind, or a virus, you need a good copy. And if that happens, the first thing you do with the surviving copy is—"

In chorus, they yelled, "Copy."

"Right! Mr. Stewart hasn't yet found an easily accessible place for storing the offsite copies. Right now he and Mrs. Nelson are sharing that responsibility. But the rest of you must see to it that they get your copies. It's your responsibility. Pay close attention to this."

After that, the Stewart employees all practiced what they'd learned the day before. Linda was available for consultation, but she didn't solve their problems, she only guided them into solving the errors by themselves.

Lunch again was catered. That was a smart move on Mr. Stewart's part. Eating together gave the study session a holiday atmosphere and was excellent for employee relations. It was a good ploy for the employees to feel they were involved together in the new program.

Jim sought Linda. He was so cordial that she wondered why he'd been rude the day before. He too wanted to show her around Waco, and he said, "I stopped off at your bed-and-breakfast, but you weren't there.''

"I went for a ride aróund Lake Waco."

"The lake's very nice for sailing. How about going and watching the races on Sunday? I would enjoy having you there.''

"You race?" How could he if he feared water?

"No, no. I watch. Safely ashore, I enjoy the sight of the boats racing. It must be a lot like flying.''

"You fly?"

Jim was rueful. "Not if I can drive.''

"We all have our fears.''

"What are yours?''

"Liars.''

He waited, with a slight smile. "Nothing else?''

"Big, black, silent trucks.''

"That sounds like a terrific nightmare.'' Jim's words belied his solemn sympathetic expression.

"It is.''

"Did you ever see Steven Spielberg's 'Duel' with the car being hunted by a truck on a California highway?''

"Once. It really set me on edge. I suppose it was because I could never see the driver. It made the truck the villain instead of a deranged man.''

Jim agreed. "It helps to know our adversaries.''

Linda wondered who were his adversaries, then heard Bob's voice at her side just as his hand took hold of her elbow. "Moving in on my territory?" he asked Jim.

Jim's eyes closed down while staying wide-open. That was interesting to witness. Linda had seen Jim's eyes change even as she automatically lifted her elbow out of Bob's hand. She had learned long ago, in an office, not to allow the least bit of casual touching. It only invited more.

She then had to defuse the "territory" word, so she changed the meaning of his word as she said in a positive way, "Jim is good at his job. It doesn't appear that he's trying to take over yours, too. But he could if you needed him."

Then she changed the subject, "It appears you are both familiar with computer usage. I'm impressed. Why were you opposed to installing computers here, Bob? I would think with knowing them as well as you seem to, you would have had them long ago."

Earnestly, Bob replied, "I didn't know there were people like you who could make it all so easy, to come here for the teaching and help with the transition of this many employees. You've not only done a good job, you've made it exciting and interesting. Teaching them to find their own mistakes and find out why they made them has been especially well done."

"You're welcome."

Jim asked, "I understand you'll be available next week if we should hit a snag?"

"Yes. That's free. No charge. I'll be in town where I can be reached. I have a beeper. And if you really need me, I'll come here. I don't believe you will. Your people are enthusiastic and quick. This is a good place to work."

Bob put in: "I have to admit that Jim is responsible for that. He's been here almost two years. My dad brought him into the firm, gave him carte blanche, and he's done a hell of a job."

Linda noted that although Bob's words appeared to be praise, they really weren't. Interesting. And with the undercurrent of tension she felt, she was glad she wasn't a Stewart employee.

By mid-afternoon Linda decided the two men were perfectly easy with one another, and it was only her vivid and unbridled imagination that had conjured any stress between the two. They spoke to each other without tact, but their words appeared not to offend either.

And speaking of offending someone, she was soon to go ho—to go back to the bed-and-breakfast where Mitch was waiting for her to have supper with him.

It really had been her fault that their emotions had gotten so steamed up. She'd just now stopped Bob from touching her. She could have done the same thing last night with Mitch. He'd given her every opportunity to keep him distanced. But when he'd put on that wild and raucous music, had she been demure and modest? No.

She'd jumped right up and let the music take her. She'd wiggled and jiggled around, acting like a wanton. That's what she'd done, all right. If she'd behaved herself, Mitch wouldn't have gotten so out-of-hand. Well, he wouldn't have tried to get out-of-hand. Actually she had led him right along, cooperating all the way. It had been a good thing Molly had turned up when she did with her glue pie.

What would have happened if Molly hadn't been so insistent in ringing that doorbell? Linda sat in the midst of those busy people at their terminals and she stared into space, considering how delicious it could have been. Her imagination soon had Mitch naked and on her bed, investigating their differences...

...when one of the warehouse men, right in front of her said, "You're something, do you know that?

Here I am all thumbs and desperate, and you just waited for me to figure it out. It was easy! I wish my kids had teachers like you.''

Linda was appalled. There she'd been daydreaming erotica, not paying any attention at all when someone had needed her help. She was very attentive for the rest of the afternoon.

During that time both Bob and Jim found time to talk to her. They were flirting, but being executives they were more subtle than some of the other men there. She could have booked dates for the next two weeks. Linda knew that their attention wasn't because she was anything special. It was because she was a stranger, therefore she would be safe for them to date. They could go with her and not become labeled as hers.

There was none who interested her, because she'd already seen Mitch. Even as awkward as it would be, she was aching to see him again. She would, of course, be distant with him. She would look at him aloofly and speak nicely, but she wouldn't fling herself on his chest and beg for his attentions.

But Linda did notice that Bob didn't collect the offsite tape when he left. So Linda made a copy and took it with her. It was a lesson they should all learn. A very important one.

So she drove ho—to the house on Premont Street. She drew up to the curb and stopped. Then she had to instruct her knees on how to be firm. She got out of the car and was walking creditably up the walk, when she heard a low, snarling cat's warning.

Their cat? She looked around and saw a crouched tricolored cat in the bushes, and their black cat was very, very, very slowly moving around, one hair's breadth at a time nearer to the back of the female.

That would be Mitch's cat, all right.

Feeling somewhat beleaguered herself, Linda felt her sympathies were with the crouching female. Linda went silently along the overgrown grass and stomped her foot at the black male, who ignored her. But the female snarled at Linda! That was a surprise. The female did *not* want to be rescued from that single-minded male.

In fact, the tricolored cat was exactly as riveted as Linda had been the night before! Linda leaned over and said to the female, "You'll regret this."

The female hissed at Linda, then darted away into the bushes with the black cat right on her tail, so to speak.

Linda demanded of the male, "Come here this minute."

And from just above her came a remarkable but amused male voice: "I don't think he will."

She turned around and looked up at Mitch, standing on the porch and looking down at her with greedy eyes.

It embarrassed Linda that he'd seen her trying to save the female from a fate worse than death. Especially since Linda had behaved as outrageously last night with another male animal who now stood above her on the porch. She couldn't think of any retort.

With nonthreatening kindness, Mitch said, "How was your day?"

Standing there, not moving, she replied automatically, "Fine." But she was remembering that because of this man her thoughts hadn't always been on her students. He was a distracting man. It was a good thing she would be going back to Dallas, before the words bed-and-breakfast took on another meaning entirely.

Then her recovering conscience mentioned that Linda had known this dangerous man for just forty-eight hours.

The whole problem with Mitch was ridiculous. Linda wished she could start over with him. Then she would be cool and in control. She would speak more carefully.

Actually, it hadn't been speech that had gotten her in trouble. It had been wild music and wild kisses and a very wildly exciting man. It had been this particular man who was watching her from the porch.

And the Smiths had said that he was shy.

She eyed him. If he was "shy" acting the way he did, what would he be like aggressive? And her shocking body clamored for an example.

Linda looked longingly back at her car, but only cowards fled. She told her feet to move, and they did that quite nicely, so she walked over to the steps and climbed them to the porch...and Mitch. To be off-putting, she said rather severely, "Both my bosses came by here and couldn't find me registered."

That wouldn't be surprising; this wasn't where she was supposed to be. "What did they want?"

She bristled a little, not wanting to reply. "Nothing."

"Ah. So they, uh, came by for no reason?"

"What did you tell them?"

"Nothing." That was true enough.

Since the two men niggled in her mind, and since Mitch must have seen them, Linda asked, "What did you think of them?"

"Why?"

"I get such feelings of antagonism between them, but they appear just abrasive-mannered. I wondered what you thought of them."

"Zero." How could he have an opinion? Not having met them, he had no idea about them.

Linda and Mitch were standing there, not moving an inch, and she had to pass Mitch to get to the front door. She took a step. Mitch should have then moved back a step if he'd been courteous, but he stood his ground. She took another step, and he turned toward her. She looked up at him, and he leaned and kissed her mouth.

Her silly mouth just puckered right up and kissed back, as if that was what it was supposed to do! And she scolded herself quite crossly that she needed some cooperation from herself to keep him at bay! Her mouth smiled.

"I missed you today," he told her. "It was such a long time to have you gone. I wondered how you were getting along."

"Fine." Her tirade that morning had left them uncomfortable with each other. It was difficult to make even casual conversation. She took another slow step to pass him, and he turned with her step. It was very like the turning of the cats. She was moving as if trying to get past, and he was blocking her.

She took another step, and he reached past her and opened the door to his spider web.

She was amazed by the entrance hall. He'd really been working. All the paper was hung on the gauzed walls. Here the woodwork was also natural wood. And it was beautiful. She gasped and smiled over her shoulder at Mitch who was following her inside. Linda exclaimed, "Beautiful! And this is the perfect place for your registration desk. I really ought to sign your book."

"I'll give it to you before you leave."

"I smell the enchiladas." She put her head back, closed her eyes and inhaled. If she hadn't acted so dumb that morning, what would they have said to each other now? Well, more than likely they wouldn't have been talking. She would probably be tightly against him with his arms holding her there, and he would be kissing her dizzy and getting quite fresh. She was disgusted with her morning's conduct and with having canceled the possibility of that.

For a woman who needed to reform, she was having a struggle getting insider cooperation.

Mitch was saying, "—up and get into something more comfortable."

He said that with a completely straight face, which indicated jeans and a pullover. So she nodded and went up the stairs. She knew he waited below, because she looked back from the landing and he was still there watching over her.

She had the best-looking backside he'd ever watched in action, and he was a connoisseur. As she looked back at him, he smiled beatifically.

She thought that he really was shy. She must not lead him astray. He was a quick learner. She could ruin him. In her bathroom, she stripped, had another cold rinse-off and shivered into her sweats. She would really need to jog if she was to survive a whole evening of his allure. She must keep her hands to herself and not flirt or invite. All that would take would be stern discipline, and she had that in ample supply.

Linda came down the stairs, and he was surprised to see her in gray sweats. "Jogging?"

"Yes. It's grueling," she lied, "to teach such a mob all day. I get very tense." Sure. She'd just day-dreamed about tearing a bed apart with Mitch Roads. That was the only stress she'd experienced that day.

"I'll go with you."

"Don't you get enough exercise wallpapering? I should think that would be exhausting."

"Different muscles," he replied easily.

He gave her a small glass of orange juice, and they went out into the overcast late-afternoon.

"Molly give you any more pies?"

"Didn't see hide nor hair all the livelong day. You may have cured her."

Cured Molly? Linda could only remember Molly standing on the porch and looking inside like a child drooling at bonbons through a shop window. Linda was glad she didn't live in that town, or her reputation would be all shot to hell.

Their run was good. Spring in Texas had an elusive smell. It might be the kinds of trees and grasses that contributed to the different fragrance. Linda was filled with a familiar nostalgia that she couldn't quite place. It was as if a poignant memory was just out of reach. She'd felt that wistfulness before, so it wasn't the thought of giving up Mitch that— She would have to give up Mitch? She'd go back to Dallas and never see him again!

She didn't remember any more of their run. She frowned a little and wondered if every spring for all her life, she would be remembering Mitch, coupled with that strange spring scent? That was rather sad, for then she might never know the genetic melancholy that she always suffered each spring. From here on out, all the rest of her days, the longing would center on Mitch instead.

When they returned to the bed-and-breakfast, Mitch gave her the choice of a hot shower downstairs or two buckets of boiling hot water to warm her tub for a deep, relaxing bath.

If she was all relaxed from a deep, hot bath, she might not be on her guard, so she chose the shower. That wasn't a particularly good idea because she thought of him naked and standing there with her, and her body loved the idea.

She scrubbed her skin with a rough towel and dressed sensibly in jeans and loose pullover.

They had the enchilada dinners from the un-marked, foil-wrapped packages; and the spicy foods were delicious. "At Stewart's, everyone loved the doughnuts. You need to tell me what they cost. I do have an expense account, you know, and my com-pany would be pleased I did this. It's good P.R."

"A trifling. I believe it was two dollars."

She laughed. "You're talking to a city woman, and I know doughnuts cost more than that. It was more like fifty for that many doughnuts. Don't try to kid a woman from Dallas."

"Tell me about Dallas."

"It's a good town. It has it all. But I must say that Waco is delightful. Given a choice, I'd—" she paused "—think people would be very happy here. There's good civic interest. I'm looking forward to flying a kite. Where do we buy them?"

"We make it."

And again, she laughed.

He watched her laugh and smiled with it. But he wondered what she'd almost said about living in Waco.

Six

So we make the kite?" Linda asked as they cleared away the dishes after supper.

"We'll have the only authentic kite there," Mitch assured her.

"What do you intend to use? Waxed vellum? Cloth?"

"Newspaper."

"You said authentic," she teased.

"What's more authentic than crossed sticks and newspaper?"

"Do you know how long there've been kites? I've been reading up on the Wind Festival. Kites have been around almost as long as man. I suppose the first kites were scraped animal skins."

Mitch nodded in agreement.

"The first known one is an Egyptian hieroglyphic made in 500 B.C. that shows a man flying a kite."

"Men aren't too different. The difference is in the tools he has." Mitch stood a length of thin half-inch board next to Linda and marked it at her height.

She shared more: "And in 200 B.C. it was recorded that a Chinese general flew a kite over his enemy's stronghold in order to figure out how far he'd have to dig a tunnel to get inside."

Mitch used clippers to cut the board. He measured the length, then measured a shorter piece and marked it. That was also clipped. He notched each end of both pieces, then measured each length and marked the centers exactly.

Linda was a fund of information. "In a competition in 1847, a kid suggested that the bridge engineers fly a kite across the Niagara River and use its string to pull across a stronger string, then tie a rope to that string and pull it across, and finally the first cable. It worked."

Mitch unwound string from a ball, waxing it between two squares of thread wax.

Linda's dissertation went on: "A hundred years ago, the Japanese regularly used giant kites to lift heavy loads to workmen at higher levels."

"Hold those steady while I wrap them." He gave her the two sticks, crossed, then began to wind the string in another cross to hold the two together. "You retain information very well."

"But only for forty-eight hours. Then it eludes me. Some bits and pieces will pop up at odd times and I'm entertained. If I have to have information, I rely on backup computer copies and a public library."

There was a yowl from behind the kitchen, and Mitch obediently went to open the door for the cat.

The cat came in, ate, and eventually joined them in the dining room, watching the kite-making with interest.

Pushing the cat aside, Mitch strung some of the string from notched end to notched end, making the diamond shape of the finished kite.

Linda commented, "I don't recall ever seeing such a kite."

"That's because you never lived in West Texas where the traditions are still honored. We can now glue on the newspaper. As you can see, the paper has been seamed to fit this size kite, and yesterday the surface was waxed on both sides to make it stronger."

He laid the paper on the floor, put the crossed sticks on top of it and moved the cat off the paper. Then he cut the paper an inch and a half larger than the string outline so that the paper could be folded over the string and glued onto it. And he moved the cat less gently off the paper.

At each of the four board ends, he folded the paper so that the ends of the boards were free. In each end, he drilled a hole. Pushing the cat aside, he strung guy strings from each of the four points to meet a centered string a foot out from the crossed middle.

Linda picked up the cat and held him out of the way. The cat hung there as if he had no backbone and was no threat to anyone. Linda figured the calico must have drained him.

Mitch explained, "This is really a wind sail. Just like that on a boat. See? It will fill with the wind and pull the kite."

"What's printed on the paper?"

"I don't know. I just took some of the widest ones."

"Will they rip apart?"

"Maybe. Sails are seamed. We can tape the paper if it does split."

"Let me see." She put the cat aside and knelt down and, reading, she crawled around the kite. "Here's an article on the Wind Festival. That's appropriate."

Mitch hunkered down. "Here's a plane crash. Is that an omen?" But he was watching her move about on hands and knees, her attention on the kite.

She shook her head. "No bad omen. Here's something about waste-dumping. That's important."

"Here's a top-level easement for a company's restrictions on air pollution. That's appropriate, too."

"Yes," she said in censure.

She was earnestly concentrated as she moved; her body was exciting his. With ease, he went down on his own hands and knees and moved counterclockwise to her crawl, and he met her nose-to-nose. He turned his head, and she held still for his kiss.

They'd been wasting a hell of a lot of time on kites, for crying out loud.

He straightened to his knees, put his hands on her body under her arms and lifted her up against him. Then he wrapped his arms around her and kissed her again. It was kissing that was the stuff of dreams, not jeweled falcons. It was the fantasy of life to hold Linda against him and kiss her as he wanted. It was also disorienting and disrupting to his whole, entire life-support system. But his attention was riveted so completely that he had a grip on reality and, of course, on Linda.

It was just a good thing that he was holding her so strongly for she was not able to function. All her strong admonitions had disintegrated. At first her only point of reality was his mouth on hers, then she began to feel his surface with her exquisitely sensitized body. And she was mesmerized. This was Sex. This was what being a woman with a man was about. This was Life's Real Purpose and—

Hold it. Just a minute here, Linda Ann Parsons. Straighten up. Behave. Cut that out. Uh. Really now. Pay attention. I know. Yes. Ahh.

She went into a sexual swoon and hung boneless in his arms, very much the way the cat had been just a while ago. She was held by Mitch and had no help at all from her rubbery knees. It was thrilling her insides to feel his chest move against hers as he breathed. She was suffocating and would probably die pretty soon, but being held like that was worth it.

There were odd background noises as Mitch turned Linda and laid her flat out on the floor. She was probably hearing her conscience utter all the warnings she'd been besieged with all her life. A concentrated, last-ditch effort . . .

Mitch jerked his head up, then rolled away from her and somehow got to his feet as the Smiths came in. Through the locked front door! *They had a key?* That was carrying friendship much, much too far.

Linda turned on her side to prop her head on one hand in order to act as if her unfocused eyes were looking around the cat at the print on the kite. Mitch had walked stiffly over to the window and was looking out into the side yard at the dusky evening.

Nick came in first, saw them playing statues and he laughed. Lee came along and looked at Mitch, then Linda and finally at Nick. She asked, "What's so funny?"

Her husband replied to her with another puzzle. "We didn't knock."

Lee didn't understand. Linda was still coping, but Mitch gave Nick a single nod.

Lee was delighted with the kite and announced they'd go along on Sunday to cheer them on, as good friends should.

Linda stretched her mouth into a semblance of a smile. The Smiths shouldn't realize that they headed her nuisance list. As she smiled, Linda heard Mitch being accepting to the intrusion of his friends. He didn't exclaim in frustration or tell them to run along and mind their own business or anything. He talked to Nick about the house, just as if any of it was Nick's business.

The Smiths had to see every single thing that had been done that day, and they did exclaim nicely and then discuss it. But then Nick and Mitch readied the paraphernalia and began papering the rest of the upstairs halls, and Lee watched with comments.

Finally Linda gave up because she'd had very little sleep the night before. Since she'd first laid eyes on Mitchell Roads, her nerves had been stretched beyond their elastic capability, and she finally understood the expression "strung out." She excused herself nicely, having been brought up to do that sort of thing, and she went to bed.

It was midnight before the owners of that house left, and Mitch went to his lonely sleeping bag to share it again with the spoiled cat.

On Saturday morning, Linda wakened to sounds. She opened her eyes almost to a slit so that she could see the clock. It was eight-thirty-three. In this reasonably civilized world, even though it wasn't Dallas, who

in hell would intrude at that time on a Saturday
morning?

She guessed it: the Smiths.

Linda lay in her bed, disgruntled, experiencing a
strong feeling of hostility toward the Smiths. Couldn't
they stay home for once? Anyone who barged in un-
announced as they did, must be pretty crass. Linda
was baffled by anyone that stupid. They didn't realize
they should not. They'd never been taught to call
ahead.

Of course, they probably felt free to drop by that
way. Mitch was never surprised to see them. He accepted that they would just open the door and walk
right on in. It was his fault. No one takes advantages
unless allowed to do so. All that Mitch had to say was:
call first.

This was wreaking havoc on her plans for seducing
Mitch. Seducing Mitch? Well, for goodness sake, she
was planning on *seducing* Mitch! That was the first
she'd known of it. A seduction. How interesting. And
this was the perfect time. She might just as well. Mitch
seemed willing, and Linda knew she'd probably never
be back to Waco. She could seduce Mitch, find out
what this was all about and leave. Like a sailor. Like
a robber. Hit-and-run.

She'd have to be quick about it. She didn't have
much time, and she didn't want Mitch to know her too
well or his feelings could become involved. He was
attracted. The seduction ought not to be too difficult.
All she needed was an opportunity. She had the whole
house and Mitch, if the Smiths would just stay home
for a night.

How was she to get the Smiths to back off and quit
being such *very* good friends? She needed to get them

to stay home without hurting their feelings. Mitch should change the lock on the door.

What possible reason could Linda give Mitch for changing his door locks? That entertained her for a while.

There was a slight tap on her door, and Linda knew Mitch had brought her coffee. Quickly she arranged the pillows and pulled her gown straight but unbuttoned two buttons, then she called, "Come in."

And Lee opened the door.

Of course. Who else?

"Are you awake enough to want a cup of coffee?"

Lee entered and looked around the room with such an expression of satisfaction that Linda thought Lee appeared...almost possessive. And Lee completely missed Linda's unwelcoming stare.

Linda said "Good morning," and adjusted her attitude. It wasn't her house and these people were Mitch's friends.

"Do you like the room?" The pregnant Lee moved carefully over and sat on the edge of the bed. There were no chairs.

There was something in the way that Lee moved that touched Linda. "Are you okay?"

"Full." Lee sat very straight. "There isn't anymore room inside my skin. Isn't this room pretty?" And she looked at Linda with a tiny, waiting smile.

Linda complied. "It's just like summer."

"I thought it would be. I love it. It would be very nice for—" she glanced at Linda "—guests."

An idea occurred to Linda. "Did you help Mitch with the decorating?"

"Uh, yes."

"It's very nice for him to have you all so interested in his—" she gestured to the room "—place."

"Mitch is one of Nick's best friends. They go back a long way. I don't know him very well. He's shy."

Since Mitch hadn't shown any real signs of shyness with *her*, Linda didn't know how to respond to that. So she just said, "He is considerate." He always watched to be sure she got upstairs okay.

"I...he has the cushions for the window seat on the landing. They...I think they look nice."

"I'm rather amazed he was accepting guests before he was finished with the whole place."

"Maybe he needs the money," Lee guessed lamely.

That made sense. "Yes. Perhaps so. I probably should pay by the day."

"I...don't believe you should do that," Lee backtracked. "He has such pride, you see, that he might be offended."

"Oh. Well, I could offer."

"I probably shouldn't have said anything. He's so shy that if he thought I had said anything, it would embarrass him."

"Then I won't."

"Good. How did things go at Stewart's Hardware?"

"Just right. They are a nice bunch of people." But there was that feeling Linda had that something was wrong at Stewart's, so she asked, "Do you know Bob and Jim?"

"I've only met Jim, but Bob is an old acquaintance. He was under his daddy's thumb for so long that I think it ruined Bob. The old man was a terror. He's recovering from apoplexy. He just about died when their payroll was shredded. Literally, he did just about die. He had a fit. There were people who witnessed it that are still spooked by what happened.

"The seizure must have been something to have seen, I would guess. Everyone there was stunned. It was so strange and tense that after the first surprise of it, people don't even mention it anymore. But everybody dreads the old man getting well and taking control back from Bob. I hear tell Bob's doing well enough. I'm glad they got the computer system."

With some pride Linda was pleased to tell Lee, "They've taken to it like ducks to water bugs."

Lee laughed. "To water *bugs*?"

"Yes. Ducks just go calmly into water, but you should see them scramble in a nest of bugs. That's the way the Stewart employees took to computers." Linda slid out of bed and said, "You can't be comfortable sitting like that. I'll get dressed and we'll go downstairs where you can be easier."

"Good. I'm glad you don't mind getting up. They won't let me do anything, and I have trouble just sitting."

"Do anything?" Linda inquired.

"Nick's been antsy to... help Mitch with the work. He's been over here since breakfast. I told him that Mitch wouldn't want to work today, but Nick didn't mind if Mitch didn't. He's...looking forward to Mitch being done with it. It's been such a big job."

Linda commented, "This is a love of a house. I wish I could have known the people who built it. It's so amazingly contrived with the walk-arounds through the rooms and closets. Really marvelous. Wouldn't it have been a great place to be a child?"

"That's what we thought, too." Lee smiled, then sobered and added lamely, "For Mitch."

"Is he planning to marry?"

"No. He's so shy. I just wonder if he'll ever marry. It would be a shame if he didn't."

That made Linda pensive. Could she seduce a shy man and maybe break his heart?

"What are your plans," Lee asked. "Are you ambitious?"

"I have a business degree and—" she gestured "—the computer training. I'd like to set up my own payroll operation. Take over the writing of checks and keeping track of employees for companies. Too much employee time is spent doing that when they could be more involved with their businesses. Like small retail stores or publicity firms. Graphic specialists. Television stations. That sort of thing. I love figures and enjoy doing that kind of work. Most people hate it. And I like helping firms set up computer systems. It makes life so much easier for them."

Lee frowned. "Then you aren't looking around for a husband?"

"Not yet."

And Lee's frown deepened.

Since there was no reason for Lee to frown, Linda asked, "Are you all right?"

"Yes. I was just thinking."

"Will you excuse me? I'll get dressed." Linda took her things into the bath across the hall, dressed and washed her face in the cold water, then returned to find her bed made and Lee waiting for her. "You made the bed?"

"No problem."

"You ought to be careful."

"That's what everybody says."

"Listen to them."

Lee grinned as she replied, "Okay."

They went down the stairs to the landing where Linda admired the purple window-seat cushions, tried them out and exclaimed, as Lee obviously wanted her to do.

Lee coaxed admiration by asking, "Aren't they rich?"

"Beautiful. And comfortable. Wouldn't you know he'd want purple here?"

"Why do you say that? Don't you really like them?"

Linda smiled. "You are loyal. I think they're just fine."

"Why did you say wouldn't I know that he would want purple?"

"I think the color would appeal to him."

"But not to you?"

"It's fine!" Linda assured Lee, thinking how to get past the need to reassure her. How strangely strident Lee was about Mitch's purple cushions.

They were met at the bottom of the steps by the hightailed cat. Linda let it out the front door. As it walked by, Linda leaned over and said, "Leave that little calico alone."

The cat leaped past Linda as if she might close the door at the last minute. Linda laughed, so the cat then sat on the porch, surveying his recently acquired territory as if there wasn't any hurry.

With distaste, Lee said, "At least this cat's a male."

"You don't like cats?"

"Not a bit. That one belongs to Mitch," Lee said emphatically.

A gorgeous male voice inquired, "What belongs to Mitch?"

And he was there.

Lee said something rather stridently that didn't penetrate Linda's hearing. Her ears had taken in Mitch's sound and her insides shivered, her skin prickled, her knees wobbled and her brain spun around inside her skull. He made her feel weird. Just his voice did all that. She managed to turn toward the sound of him, and she floated off the floor an inch or two. She just . . . floated.

He stared at her.

She smiled dewily and said, "Hello."

He nodded seriously, in tiny, tiny nods that were more tremor than nod.

Lee was fascinated. She went off to find Nick and tell him what she'd just witnessed. Nick *wasn't* at all surprised, which was a big disappointment to Lee. "Why didn't you tell me?" Lee demanded of her husband in indignation.

"I thought you knew." That old dodge.

Back in the front hall, Mitch took Linda's hand and tugged her floating body to his, put his arms around her like a boa constrictor and kissed her with shiveringly concentrated lust.

She recognized it was a powerful drive that swamped him. She'd never seen that before and she was a little amazed. While she had planned on seducing him for curiosity's sake, he wanted her. He intended *getting* her, and if she didn't want to be had, she'd better get out of there. She made her voice speak in order to protest this maelstrom of wanting she knew was boiling in him, and her voice said, "Have you had breakfast?" She blinked to hear such a wimpy sentence come out of her mouth and tried again. "Did you sleep last night?" What had made her ask that?

"I could have, but you'd locked your door."

Shocked that this shy man could be so blatant, she opened her mouth and this deliciously intimate chuckle came out. She listened amazed that she could make such a sound.

He kissed her, and she didn't mind at all. But when he lifted his mouth to gasp, she asked, "Why are your friends here again?" And her voice sounded peeved.

"Nick's helping do it."

"What?"

"Hmmm?" Mitch murmured the questioning sound.

"What's he helping do?"

"Who?"

"Nick," Linda clarified. "What's he helping d—"

"The house."

"Oh."

He kissed her again.

Thoroughly. Marvelously. Deliciously. Thrillingly. Everything. She said, "They're here a whole lot."

"It's their house."

She figured he meant the Spanish saying and asked, "My house is your house?"

Not quite tracking, he inquired, "Do you have a house?"

"An apartment."

"You ought to live here."

"Yes. It's lovely. You are so clever. I love the purple cushions on the landing."

"What purple cushions?"

"Those on the landing."

With her plastered down his length, he carried her over to the bottom of the stairs and looked up past her head. There were purple cushions on the landing window seats. "Um-hum. Nice."

"I'm hungry."

"What do I get if I feed you?"

"A tip?"

"What sort of tip?" He watched her with hot eyes.

"Fifteen percent?"

"Of what?"

"The price?"

"That allows me liberties. I can put my hands there, and here. And I get to kiss you like this."

She knew that her eyes spun when he lifted his scalding mouth from her ravaged one. His breath was harsh and his body as hard as rock. With very slow words, she whispered, "You're not supposed to do that until I've eaten. You took your tip before I had anything to eat." She was looking a little cross-eyed since he was so close and she was having so much trouble focusing. Then she frowned. "I thought you were shy."

"I am."

She had to think about a reply.

So with one arm tightly across her upper back and the other hand spread out below the middle of her back, again holding her down his body, he carried her into the kitchen. There, he propped her against the counter, in his way, so that he had to brush close against her and he could kiss her quite easily and often.

She had no idea what she ate. He fed her and kissed her. And she took food from his lips as he leaned against her, trapping her hard against the counter with his needy body.

"This isn't a good idea," she managed to say once when her mouth was free. "They could come in here any time."

"It's the best idea I've ever had, and I told Nick I'd kill him if he came in here."

"Lee's pregnant."

"I know."

"You can't push her around."

"Nick will handle her."

"He already has." And she listened to herself laugh real sultry. She could do that? How astonishing. His answering laugh was very low and almost silent and wicked as all get out. It sent shivers up her back, under her armpits and over her squashed breasts, down her arms, through her stomach and intimately along inside her thighs. His laugh did that.

"I want you." His voice was husky.

That again. "I noticed."

"You won't escape much longer."

"I, uh, thought innkeepers had to be aloof."

He ran his hands up from her hips to the sides of her squashed breasts and he very sneakily rubbed his body into hers.

She played with the hair on the back of his head. When had her hands gotten up there? She pulled her wobbly head back and managed, "Don't. You must not. It would be very embarrassing if they came in here."

"They won't."

"But I'll have to face them, and they will *know* we've been . . ."

"Been?"

"Fooling around."

"Yeah. Like it?"

"Y-e-e-e-s-s-s."

His laugh was so shaky and low and naughty that she almost threw him over her shoulder and carried him upstairs to her room, to pitch him on her bed and bolt the door. The only reason she didn't was because she just wasn't physically organized. If she was sure that she could count on her various appendages and muscles behaving, she would have tried. But she wasn't at all coordinated.

Without Mitch and the cabinets holding her upright, she'd be flat on the floor. This must be what they meant about a round-heeled woman. She went down easily.

But she wasn't easy. She was twenty-seven and still intact. How had she lasted all these years without once being tempted this way? Now she was a shambles after knowing this man only sixty-five hours. See? She *could* still function. At least mathematically. Otherwise she was a zero.

With her backside trapped tightly between his body and the cabinet, he gathered her closer, curling his body to hers as he hugged her and kissed her witless.

Then he left her propped against the counter as he walked around for a while, rubbing a hand on his chest and practicing breathing in and out and having trouble doing it.

Then Lee called, "Mitch, come help Nick."

The pair in the kitchen could hear Nick's rumbling protest Lee's command.

Lee said to Nick, "He needs to help."

Mitch hollered back, "I'll be there in just a minute. I have to settle my guest."

His guest just watched him, her eyes vacant, her face vapid, her body not worth a plugged nickel.

He came back to her and put his hard hand along her jaw with his thumb under it. Holding her steady, he told her, "I'm gonna get you."

And she laughed in the way that she hadn't known she could.

Seven

They found Nick upstairs in the front corner bedroom, putting up wallpaper. "This is trickier than you make it look," he told Mitch.

Linda wondered why Mitch should let Nick interfere with the work. Why didn't Mitch just tell his friend to cut it out and leave things be?

But tolerant Mitch said, "It's no big deal. We'll have it done in time."

Linda wondered: In time for what? Probably another guest. And she found she didn't really want another guest there, sharing their breakfasts and dinners and being underfoot, very like the Smiths always seemed to be.

Nick said positively, "I'd like to get this done today."

"No problem."

Linda was a little indignant that Mitch would give up, just like that, and do it Nick's way. It was Mitch's bed-and-breakfast. What if Mitch wanted the weekend free?

So during the morning Linda and Lee looked around through the house. Linda began the "let's pretend," saying where she would put things, adding "If it was my house."

She found that Lee had very firm ideas about what she'd do in the house. It was as if Lee had planned it all along, because she didn't hesitate—she *knew* how she wanted it. Linda figured that was because Lee had helped Mitch with the decorating scheme and felt a little possessive.

The two men finished not only the upstairs corner room, but the little one next to it. That room had plain paper with a blue border of rabbits. A child's room. Blatantly it was a child's room. With only seven rooms to rent, why would Mitch make one so definitely a child's room? He was hard to figure out.

Oddly enough, Lee had brought along lunch. That made Linda realize that the Smiths had just assumed that they would be there all morning. All day? Lee had enough food for everyone. There was home-fried chicken, slaw, potato salad, rolls and apple pie. The great American picnic. And while both women had their fair share, the men finished it all. Even the crumbs. It was amazing.

"What sort of baby do you want, other than a healthy one?" Linda asked the Smiths. And the way she questioned showed how distanced she was from families.

She learned that the Smiths were still debating over which it would be. He wanted a girl, and she wanted a boy.

"We both just really want the baby," Nick told Linda. "We're going to call the kid Mitchell or Michelle. Mitch is going to be the godfather."

So the godfather-to-be stuffed roll pieces in his cheeks and talked like Marlon Brando as Don Corleone, but with Mitch's blond hair and green eyes he just didn't look the part.

While the men tidied up from the picnic, the two women went upstairs to lie down on Linda's bed in order to force Lee to rest, and they talked lazily.

Lee asked, "Tell me about Dallas. Do you like living there?" And she asked, "Are you from a big family?"

"I've never lived anywhere but Dallas, and there's just my mother and me. My daddy divorced my mother when I was twelve, and he married another woman. It was a very tough time for us all. He grieved so over the whole thing. Mother was just sick, and I was appalled.

"My mother had married my daddy right out of high school, and they lost their first two babies. She'd been a housewife all that time. With the divorce, she had to get a job but she had no training at all. Then Daddy's new wife got pregnant and had twins the first shot. That made my mother bitter.

"So we didn't get much support money. Mother had a lot of little jobs. She worked her tail off, keeping us going. Then I got scholarships, we both worked and she went to school, too. She's a job counselor for women, and I'm very proud of her. But she's had a really hard time of it."

Gently supportive, Lee suggested, "She's probably achieved a very solid life."

"The hard way," Linda agreed pensively. "What about your family?"

"We've lived here since our ancestors first moved in on the Huaco Indians. I have a big family and so does Nick, that's why we bought such a big house. Although the family's scattered, they do visit."

"I'd like to see your house sometime."

Lee said a vague, "Yes."

Linda gestured to include everything. "This house is just perfect. Mother and I have always lived in apartments. It's wonderful to be in a house."

Lee said another, "Yes."

They spoke of experiences and people they'd known, as they became acquainted. When Lee was rested, the two women went downstairs and the four wandered through the house, admiring the finished rooms. It was then that Linda saw a cherry drop-leaf table and four matching chairs had appeared in the dining room.

Linda put her hand on the table and asked Mitch, "Where did these come from?"

"The Smiths had them brought here for the house." What he said was true.

Linda scolded, "Those are much too good to put in here. How amazing you would lend them so casually."

The Smiths exchanged a brief look and Lee said, "It's nice to have them here." So she didn't lie, either.

Then in the living room there were now four easy chairs, another lamp and a coffee table. They were lovely things from Nick's and Lee's families.

Linda asked, "How can you spare four such precious chairs this way?"

"We have no room for them where we are," Lee explained.

"Well, while it's nice for Mitch right now, you ought not to leave such lovely things to be used by strangers at a bed-and-breakfast."

Lee agreed, "No." Then Lee told her that all their friends were coming over very shortly. "They're all bringing furniture." That was true; Lee just didn't mention that it was Smith's furniture.

So that day the Smiths moved their things into their own house as Linda watched in some surprise. The movers were all sorts of people who were around Mitch and Nick's age. They managed to imply that the furniture was all donated. They said it was "from storage," which was true.

The people were friends and in on the sham of the bed-and-breakfast and avidly interested in Linda. They couldn't hide their smiles over her being fooled, but that just made them appear friendly. And nobody let the cat out of the bag, although the resident cat was there and in charge, darting ahead of the carriers and watching the placement of the furniture with interest.

The first pieces to arrive were the ones that went into Linda's room. A large dresser with a mirror. A lowboy that matched. There was a lady's small armless rocker and pictures were hung on the walls. It became a beautiful guest room.

All but Lee carried things into the house. There were people hanging drapes at the long landing windows, and people laying rugs and furniture at Lee's direction.

There were a good many shirtless men who lifted things and carried them. But Linda saw only Mitch. He was magnificent. His muscles bulged, his skin filmed with sweat and he did more than his share. He would catch her looking at him and would wink or smile at her.

Molly came to see what was going on, and Linda saw her talking to some of the men. Linda wondered if Molly was offering them glue pies.

Soon there were glass-fronted bookcases in the upper hall at the top of the stairs and a quite remarkable library table was placed in the middle of the rug laid on that floor. Downstairs, drapes appeared that could be closed against the window-peeping Molly.

In the newly papered front corner bedroom was laid a big, old, worn Persian rug. Then a beautiful antique suite of furniture was placed there. Marble-topped dressers and a commode. A lovely lounge chair and an accommodating rocker. A highboy. And a coat tree.

And in the child's room, the furniture put into place was for a very young child. A baby. It was as if... as if the *Smiths* could move right into that suite of rooms. They'd move in? Well, it wouldn't surprise Linda one bit. They could do that. As it was, they were always coming into the house as if they owned it. They probably were going to move right on in. Well, damn.

She asked Mitch, "Are Nick and Lee moving in?"

He grinned as if in relief. "They sure could. There's lots of room."

He wouldn't mind.

So Mitch found the opportunity to tell the Smiths that Linda wondered if they'd planned to move in, and he'd told her they probably would, so they could!

The Smiths found that unbelievably droll.

With everything moved in and placed in the finished rooms, the friend-movers stayed that evening for a housewarming—an *inn*-warming. There was that scattered correction and they all laughed so cheerfully.

Mitch held Linda's hand as he became acquainted with the movers and Linda noted that Mitch handled himself well with strangers. Why did Lee consider him shy?

They had a good time, so it was very late when the last of the guest movers left. By then, Linda had excused herself and gone to bed. So, even earlier, had Lee.

The Smiths moved their personal things in on Sunday. Nick and Mitch did that with some help from Linda. It was a little hectic. Lee would *not* sit down or let anyone else do anything without a big argument. And losing the arguments, she cried.

Linda was dismayed. That the Smiths would move in was bad enough, but that Lee was upset was terrible. She had reluctantly become fond of Lee.

Linda, who was a little literal, decided the Smiths' finances were so strained that they had to make this move, and taking advantage of Mitch's hospitality distressed Lee. Linda told Lee, "It's okay. Things will work out. This is only temporary. Quit worrying."

And Lee gave Linda a peculiar stare.

The men efficiently fixed lunch from Mitch's magic freezer and some leftovers from the inn-warming party the night before. They told Linda, "Sit on Lee. She's getting too tired."

Linda went to Lee, who was in the living room and looked rather weepy. Linda told the very pregnant woman, "Now how am I supposed to sit on you when there's no room on your lap?"

Lee smiled but the tears flowed.

Linda's only reference point was the fact the Smiths had had to move into their friend's inn. She knew nothing about pregnant women, so she said, "You mustn't cry. These things happen to lots of families."

Lee looked amazed, then she laughed.

Linda thought the strange reaction was because Lee was pregnant.

Mitch and Nick came to the door of the living room and beamed at Linda. "How'd you make Lee laugh?"

"I'm not sure."

That only made Lee laugh harder, and the men were carried along. Then Lee gasped, "Linda said this happens...in...in lots of...families!"

Being literal, Linda wasn't a stranger to not understanding some humor, so she let it slide, but the men roared with laughter.

Nick cautioned Lee to eat sparingly. She wasn't hungry anyway, and she only picked at her food.

Linda thought she'd heard somewhere that pregnant women were voraciously hungry and frowned at Nick for telling his wife not to eat very much. She looked over to the side to hide her annoyance at such a bossy man, and there was the kite against the wall. "Are we going to the Wind Festival?"

Lee brightened and said, "Yes!"

Nick and Mitch were doubtful. Linda knew they were tired, but Lee was pushing to go.

So they did go out to Speegleville Park, and it was a marvelous afternoon. A perfect spring day with just the right amount of wind. Their kite was praised for being a classic, and it did fly. The tail had been a problem. Because there weren't any suitable rags, Mitch had to sacrifice a shirt. He knew exactly how to fly that kite. Linda watched Mitch, not the kite; he watched her and the kite. When his head was tilted up, she knew it flew.

She studied how Mitch moved. He was so marvelously male in his movements. He was in control of everything he did. And she remembered him that morning, shirtless, lifting things, smiling at her mesmerized face or winking when he went by her.

There were a lot of people at Speegleville Park, thousands, but it wasn't a jam. There was plenty of room for the rides, the Frisbee-throwing, soap-bubble blowing and sailing contests. It was a lighthearted day.

With Lee so pregnant, they had to limit their participation to the kite-flying and listening to the concert. Lee was tired from being prevented from helping with the move, and Nick felt she shouldn't walk too much.

Then the Smiths insisted that Mitch and Linda should see the Texas Ranger Museum. Mitch had an ancestor who'd been a Ranger who had fought Mexican rustlers from across the border, and Comanche Indians who were trying to get all the invaders off their land.

So it was Mitch who told the favorite Ranger story about Bill McDonald. "There was a call for help from a town where rioting had been going on for days. The local law-enforcement officers were stymied, so they sent a wire to the Rangers. When the train pulled into town, one Ranger got off. The locals said, 'There's only one of you?' And the Ranger replied, 'There's only one riot.' And by golly, he solved it all by himself.''

Then Mitch admitted the tale was an unproven legend, and could have been based on a niggling grain-of-sand truth to puff up the well-earned, incredible Ranger reputation.

As they walked around the exhibits, Linda placed Mitch in all the diorama displays. He was such a man.

From the museum they drove down the road to look at the preserved Waco suspension bridge, now used only for pedestrian traffic. Nick said the bridge had been started just after the War Between the States, which the Yankees mislabel a civil war. The toll bridge was finished in 1870 to accommodate the stage road on an extension of the Chisholm Trail. The bridge replaced a ferry that was often delayed due to floods and storms.

''They had ferried the cattle?'' asked the rather literal Dallas native.

''No.'' Nick didn't laugh. ''Just stagecoaches, wagons and people. The cattle had swum across; but with the bridge, the cattle could be herded across. Saved time and sweat, that way.

''The bridge was the first one built over the mighty Brazos River,'' Nick explained, ''The engineer was from New York, the same engineer who later built the Brooklyn Bridge. So what he did was, he *practiced* on the Brazos.''

Afterward, they went back to the house. The cat came up to the porch and went in with them. Linda looked around from the front door into the other rooms and up the stairs. It was strange to see it looking more finished. The drop cloths had been taken away, the floors cleaned and rugs had been put down.

There was a nicely worn runner on the stairs. At the bottom of each riser was a brass rod holding the runner in place. The drapes changed the empty look, and the furniture was elegantly suited to that type of house. The pieces looked at home.

The foursome had soup and sandwiches for supper, and they were contented before a house-warming fire of wood scraps.

Linda said the day had been special. "I enjoyed the concert, especially. The idea of a Wind Festival is just charming."

Nick told her, "Then you ought to come back the end of April for the Brazos River Festival. Historic-homes tours, arts-and-crafts, art auction, games, the Cotton Palace pageant, a bunch of things. It's really something."

"It sounds nice. I'll have to see if Mitch has a room free for then."

"I'd find a place for you. Don't worry." He gave her such a pleasant, innkeeper's smile. But his eyes were wicked.

Lee nodded in agreement to finding her a place to stay. She told Linda, "It's been so nice to be with you yesterday and today. I'm glad there was the— That you were Mitch's first guest. I think you're good for him. He hasn't seemed quite so shy today."

Shy. Mitch didn't guffaw or even smile, but he had to bite his lower lip. Shy? He couldn't keep his hands off Linda. But then, she invited that. She leaned against him without knowing she did that. She touched him. She smiled at him. And she watched to see if he heard what she said and was interested.

He was surely interested.

He wanted to be her shirt. He wanted to be the chair she sat on. He wanted to be the light from the lamp that fell on her. He wanted her with a fire that was just about to burn him up.

Lee gasped.

Nick asked anxiously, "Are you all right?"

"Just a twinge."

"What . . . sort of twinge?"

"It's been going on all day. Little ones. They're getting pretty regular."

Nick went white.

Mitch grinned.

Linda stared. Lee was going through with it. Well, of course she would. How else?

Nick said, "I'll go phone the doctor."

Lee objected, "For Pete's sake, have you forgotten everything we've learned? It's not yet."

Then Nick got a chair from the dining room and sat in front of Lee and held both of her hands.

She said, "Don't hover. I'm sure this is just from being so tired."

"Lie down."

"I'm too restless."

All three hovered. They did try not to, but they did hover. Lee was surprisingly patient with them, and she turned very tender toward Nick, which made him leak tears. She teased him, and Linda watched, touched by their love.

In an aside, Mitch said to Linda, "Pay attention."

"Why?"

"You'll get a crash course in birthing and—"

"This is real! You're making a joke of it."

"I should wring my hands? I've delivered a lot of young 'uns." Dogs, sheep and one foal.

"Oh. Well, then it would be different for you. I've never even been around a cat." She paused before she added, "But that might be possible soon, with that little calico our cat's been around."

He heard the "our" and smiled. "You can be mid-wife when the time comes."

"I won't be here."

"Wanta bet?"

"I'll be through at Stewart's this week."

"If you can come back for the Brazos River Festival, you can come back for the calico's delivery. It's only a hundred miles."

"I don't have a car, and it's too expensive to fly."

"I'll come get you."

"By then, the calico would be through with the whole thing."

"You could be in on the naming session. We have to name our cat."

By the small scrap fire, Linda saw the cat close his eyes to conceal his humor. She said to the others, "This is a good time. What shall we name him?"

"Gato." Mitch grinned. "It's Spanish for cat, and this was originally Spanish land."

Her attention distracted, Lee corrected, "It was Indian before then. What did the Indians call themselves before we named them as Indians?"

"By their tribes' names," Nick replied. "Waco was named for the Huaco people who lived here before we came."

Lee suggested, "The cat looks like a villain. Let's name him Jack the Ripper."

Linda disagreed. "You can't encourage misconduct. Give him a name to live up to. Like Livingstone or Byrd or Perry."

Mitch stuck to his suggestion. "He's adventurous enough, as it is. Let's name him Gato."

There was no objection, so they tried it out on the cat, who yawned.

Lee accused her houseguest, "You've been calling him that all along, right?"

"Yeah, but I thought you all would be interested in helping to name our cat."

"It is not 'our' cat, it's yours." Lee was just a bit strident. Then she gasped and put her chin to her chest and breathed.

Nick was riveted. "You can call the cat whatever you want, but I'm going to call the doctor."

"Okay," Lee said in a very small voice.

It wasn't long before they all went to the hospital. The families were called and some gathered. The nurses were cheerful and calming. "First babies take a while," they said. But they had figured without Lee's last two days' activities. Either that, or Lee just wasn't one to fool around. They barely got her prepped when the doctor arrived, he said, just in time to catch the kid.

The gathered clans got to see him almost right away. He was a lusty, fist-clenched boy who yelled and stuck out his lower lip, which trembled. And everyone ohh-ed and aww-ed and laughed in the weepy-helpless wonder of it all.

Nick held his new son and told the child, "Don't worry, everything's under control. You got us."

Someone let Linda hold the baby, and she was pet-rified. She looked down at the new little citizen and said, "Hello." It seemed appropriate. He squinted at her with a frown.

In her ear, Mitch said, "The reason he's scowling that way is, he realizes he's too young for you and he feels cheated."

So Linda looked up at Mitch to smile at him, and someone took the baby away. Little Mitch. And she asked the godfather, "What if you want to name a son Mitchell? You and the Smiths are such good friends, the kids would see each other all the time and it would be confusing for them."

"No problem." His favorite reply. "The kids would have different last names. However, I've never particularly cared for my name. And on top of that, I was called Rocky forever. So my kid would be Dusty or Sandy or something like that."

"Rocky?"

"Yeah. Rocky Roads. But that was before Stallone made Rocky so formidable."

"I think Rocky suits you very well," she told him. "Not as the film character, but as you. You're hard as rocks."

He grinned faintly and looked at her from under heavy eyelids. It was a very smug look.

By then, the crowd of kin was edging around them to get their time with the baby. So Linda and Mitch waved to the new parents and edged on out of the room.

There wasn't a handy place open at that time of night on a Sunday, so they went back to the pseudo bed-and-breakfast to celebrate. The cat went outside as they came in the door. And they were actually alone in that big house. Mitch found a bottle of wine and opened it. They fixed some snacks and settled back in the living room with the tiny, renewed fire.

They clinked their crystal glasses that Mitch had bought that first night, and they drank a toast to the new little Smith.

"Linda, I think you ought to quit your job."

"W-what?"

"I just think that's so, so I mentioned it. I think that you oughta move to Waco and let me court you. This is a good town. It's more closed in with people and buildings than it is out west of here, but Waco's a nice place for us to get to know each other and see what happens."

"You want an upstairs maid for the bed-and-breakfast."

He laughed. "No."

"Who *is* going to do your cleaning?"

"Not you."

"That's a good attitude." She looked at him. "But you're trying to lure me here. Why?"

"You're not that dense."

"Tell me why," she invited.

"I want you."

"That's not good enough."

"Oh, yes it is, and I can show you. Come over here on the sofa."

"I learned, very young, not to sit on sofas with young men. It's a dangerous pastime."

"Somebody jumped you?"

"No. I never sat on the sofa with anyone."

"Never?" He watched her.

"Never."

"Well, you might just as well get on over here." He gave a long-suffering sigh. "You got a lot to learn."

Now how was she supposed to go over there and sit by him? He would think she wanted him to...that she was...that she wanted... Well, she did, didn't she? So she said, "I would like a little more wine."

"You'll have to come over here. I couldn't get up if my life depended on it. I've worked my tail off these last couple of days, and I'm dead on my feet."

So she was safe? Rats.

Eight

Since Mitch was completely frazzled and no threat at all, Linda got up from her chair and went to the coffee table by the sofa to pour herself a little more wine.

Showing no signs of the exhaustion he'd claimed, Mitch stood up with consummate ease, took Linda's glass from her nerveless fingers, set it aside and wrapped her in his muscled arms against his hard chest.

She liked being squashed up against him that way, and she moved a little so that her breasts rolled against him. How had she known to do that? She felt her face flush with her boldness, but he kissed her, and she helped with that.

He sat back down on the sofa, sprawled, with her stretched along his body and hanging off the couch in a very unusual position.

She opened her mouth to demur, and he kissed her again in a lovely squishy way. He *really* kissed her, and he made sounds of pleasure. With her so precariously balanced between his body and the floor, she knew that if she didn't hold on to him she would slide off.

In order to make him hold her more closely, she allowed herself to slide down him, just a little, and he groaned as he closed his arms very tightly around her. Then just as slowly, he put his hands under her arms along her body and very slowly tugged her back up him.

The experience was like nothing she'd ever encountered. And she was very pleased that it bothered him, too. She wiggled a little to get more comfortable. And he gasped, clutching her as he curled his body and parted his knees so that the lower part of her body fell through his lap. His tightened thighs saved her from sliding on down to the floor.

She was trapped. He kissed her again like a starving man, and she cooperated fully. She wiggled and strained to get back up the part of him she'd lost in the maneuver. He breathed loudly through his nose as he held still for her exquisite torture.

"You siren," he accused.

"You think I'm loud?" she murmured, her mouth blindly seeking his and kissing his chin.

He allowed her to find his mouth and shivered as she kissed him, hot and sweet. He still had his hands under her arms, his thumbs in front of her shoulders, the heels of his hands pressing her breasts together as she strained to move upward on his chest, on his body.

He allowed her struggle, holding her, preventing her success with tightened thighs and hard hands. He listened to her sounds of frustration, and he gloried in the fact that she was trying to entice him.

With skill, he turned her and lifted her over to lie flat on her back on the sofa. Then he swung over her and reversed their positions so that he lay on her chest, his hips between her thighs and his mouth on hers. Holding her there, relishing her with all his senses, he about lost his mind.

She tasted delicious, her mouth was so soft and sweet. The skin under her ear felt so tender to his gently gnawing teeth and touching tongue. She sounded as if she was eager for him, her breath was quickened and there were the little throat sounds she made. His hands were on her, and she felt completely female. Her skin was so soft and smooth, very different. She looked as beautiful lying under him as he'd dreamed she would. And she smelled hot. Ready. She smelled like a woman should: sweet, musky, ready.

He moved so that his back was to the back of the sofa. With shaky hands, he pulled her blouse up and peeled it off over her head. She wore a bra that fastened in the back, and that complicated things. He turned her toward him, as he struggled to get rid of it.

Again he had to use all five senses in appreciating her. He felt, tasted, looked. He heard the silken sound of his hand moving on her. And he buried his face against her to inhale her special scent. He closed his eyes against the wave of passion that washed through him, riveting him, his body, his attention, his need.

Linda wasn't as sure about what she wanted, but whatever it was she was willing. Her hands pulled at him, her mouth wanted to be on him. She burrowed her face into the side of his throat and groaned in gasps as she tried to get closer.

He couldn't get much closer, since he was lying on top of her with his hot desire pressed against the apex of her legs.

The inside of her body felt very different, and she was aware that she was being unpardonably reckless with him. She was helping. She was encouraging him to lustfulness. She was doing all the forbidden things. And she went right on luring him into forsaking the boundaries.

Their bodies trembled and shivered. They steamed as they gasped. Their breaths were hot and ragged, their hands stiff and scrubbing. He was out of his shirt. Then he slid off her shoes and jeans. There was only the barrier of her nothing-lace panties.

"Linda..." He was trying to brake.

"Hurry."

He made a hoarse sound.

"Mitch..."

"Honey..."

"I can't undo your belt."

That concentrated his scattering thoughts but not to her advantage. He took off his trousers and heard her gasp.

In their hurry, the fragile lace of her panties ripped, and that made him hesitate as he tried to figure out how that had happened. Then the panties were on the floor, and their bodies were back against one another feeling the difference.

He knew he needed to be sure, so he again said, "Honey..." But his breathing was rasping by then, he was sweating and he had her almost where he wanted her. And he wanted her. He surely did.

"Mitch," she begged and, pinned by him, she wiggled as much as she could.

He kissed her almost to oblivion. His tongue gave her warning as it thrust and swirled, and his hands held and squeezed and molded her. Then he sat up, sought his trouser pocket and pulled out a foil packet. He managed to tear it open and donned the protection for her.

She watched the preparation in some suspended amazement, never having seen that done, and she waited in a breathless way almost as if time stopped.

He came back to her, kissed her again, making soothing sounds of male reassurance as he gently took her.

Even though she'd warned him, he hadn't really thought she was inexperienced—so he was surprised. He snapped up his head and looked at her.

She was also surprised. It showed in her widened eyes, and she said, "Oh!"

His muscles all were so rigid that he shuddered as he hung over her, panting, waiting, not quite knowing if he should go ahead in one plunge or if he should be more careful. He'd never read anything that would give a man any idea of how to proceed under such circumstances.

He eased into her carefully. His teeth gritted, his muscles jumped but he controlled himself as well as he could. He was about to pull away so that he could get back his control, when her hands went to his back to pull him closer, and her legs wrapped around his hips!

He burst. That's what it felt like. His dam burst and relief flooded him. He collapsed on top of her with a soul-wrenched groan of spent anguish. How could a guy have so little control? He levered up shakily onto his elbows in self-disgust and looked down into her face.

She was wide-eyed and excited as she waited for what came next.

Quivering like gelatin, his sweat hot and beading his forehead, he eased from her and slid off the sofa to the floor, a ruined bruin.

She turned over on her stomach and looked over the side to ask, "Why did you quit? I really didn't mind it, you know. I don't think it would hurt at all if you did it again."

"In a while. I need some rest."

She sat up and watched him in great interest. "You're fascinating."

"I can't tell you how embarrassed I am that I couldn't control myself better. You are so hot that, Linda, I wanted you so bad that I couldn't stop. As soon as I settle down a little, I'll make love to you. I've just got to catch my breath a minute. Golly Moses, you *wrecked* me."

"I'm not too sure what I did."

"You're alive and you kissed me."

"I believe I did more than just kissing."

He grinned and managed to lift a hand clear up and put it on her knee. He patted the knee and said, "You sure did do more than that. For an amateur, you're dangerous. What will you be like with practice?"

"How much...practice have you had?"

"Uh, none. Nope. This was my first time, too."

"Now, wait a minute."

He made an X on his hairy chest. "I don't remember any other woman seducing me that way. I've been an innocent from clear out yonder in West Texas, where there aren't any wild and woolly city women who lure men onto wicked couches for carnal knowledge."

She laughed. She leaned her head back, with its tumbled hair falling down her naked back, and she laughed the most heady male-attention-getting laugh he'd ever heard in all his days. He watched her and he grinned at her because she could be teased!

He said, "When I can make it up the stairs, I want you in my sleeping bag. I've been dreaming about you being in a sleeping bag with me all my life."

"Five days."

"Well, before then I knew you were around somewhere. I just hadn't located you. When you came up on the porch that day, it was as if . . . it was time. You had come to me."

"Your first guest."

Then he remembered that he'd tricked her. He'd forgotten for just that minute that she didn't realize this was the Smiths' house. It was their furniture, so he'd relaxed his guard.

She was saying, "—bad that they didn't have one more bed for you."

"Oh, they did. I'll put the sleeping bag on top of that. Then your bones won't be hammered against the floor."

"Will Nick be back tonight? I'd hate for him to walk in right now." She leaned down from the sofa and stretched a hand for her shirt on the floor.

He stopped her, cupping the weight of her hanging breast. "Are you enticing me?"

"I'm afraid Nick will come back—"

"He's staying with Lee and Little Mitch, and sleeping in their hospital room until they come home. It's a family bonding. Also he really loves Lee, and he can't stand to be away from her. We have the house to ourselves. Do you realize that kid will be Little Mitch

until he gets as big as me then he'll be Young Mitch
and I'll be Old Mitch?''

And darned if she didn't laugh again. Then she lay
flat on her stomach, sleekly, femininely naked on the
sofa, with one leg bent up and that foot against the
back of the sofa. She looked luscious, her bottom was
firm mounds, her legs smooth and slender, her back
narrow, her breasts softly squashed by the sofa pillow. Her hair was tumbled around her head and
shoulders. She used her far hand as the pillow for her
cheek while she watched him. Then she reached her
free hand down toward him, her arm lovely and
smooth, and she lay that hand on him as she said, ''I'll
call you Rocky.''

He immediately put his hand on top of hers and
pressed it down on him as he said, ''You're a wicked
and tempting woman, Linda Parsons.''

He shifted and effortlessly turned his marvelous
body until he knelt beside her, looking down at her.
She turned her upper torso so that she looked up at
him, and they filled their sight with each other in serious regard.

He leaned to gently kiss her swollen mouth. And her
hands moved to the back of his head. He said, ''This
time we go a little slower. But I'd like us to be upstairs
in my room and in that sleeping bag.''

''I've never been camping.'' She lay on her back,
her hair spread out under her head, her pink-tipped
breasts a feast for his eyes, and she was unself-
conscious. ''Is a sleeping bag big enough for two?''

''If the two are very, very friendly.''

''How friendly?''

''Hand in glove?''

''Ahh. I see.''

"You'll feel, too, just wait. Get up, sweetheart, I could have carried you one-handed a while ago, but I'm somewhat depleted. You'll have to make the stairs on your own."

She confessed, "I seriously considered carrying you up those steps once or twice."

"Why didn't you tell me that!"

"I thought you'd be shocked."

He coaxed, "Shock me."

"Carry you upstairs?"

"I'll get upstairs for you, but then what did you mean to do with me?"

She guessed, "I believe you already know."

"Let's go practice."

They were smart enough to gather their discarded clothing and turn out the lights. They whispered and snickered as they went up the stairs, teetering dangerously and pausing on the steps as they slid their hands along one another and kissed.

Linda was in a constant blush for she was so bold. She couldn't believe her hands were doing such things or that her mouth was so greedy. That was bad enough but, for a shy man, Mitch was being excessively bold.

On the landing he sat down on the purple cushions to rest, saying, "Stairs are a wicked invention for a depleted man."

She stood watching him. With a brilliant inspiration he asked that she walk on up the stairs. The reality of his dream was to watch her walk upstairs naked.

Since it was dark and her back was to him, she didn't feel quite so displayed, so she readily obeyed and went up. The next thing she knew, he was up those steps and had her pulled back close against him. His hands were squeezing her breasts as he rubbed his face in the curve of her shoulder where it met her throat, and he groaned as if in terrible pain.

She was reminded that like love and hate, pleasure and pain are close, so her sympathies were captured. He hurt. Against some opposition on his part, she turned and put her arms around him, and his steely muscled arms bonded her to his iron body. Only then did she understand the masculine strength, and for a fleeting minute she felt a flutter of being a captive.

At that very second his arms loosened and he asked, "Too tight?"

What signal had he gotten? How had he known? But she felt almost abandoned by his loosened arms. Then she thought of the marvelously constructed hide-and-seek house. She pulled free of his arms and said, "Count to one hundred." Then she fled.

In that house in the dark, it was really cat-and-mouse. She skittered; he made no pretense at first of being quiet as he followed and stalked, but he was soon silent. She almost giggled in her sudden danger. In a corner of a closet, she too was silent, untrapped, with retreat either way. She strained her ears, listening for him. She heard him in the bathroom downstairs and relocated.

It was quickly silent again. A board creaked, and she slid away into another room. She walked around the edge of the room where the boards creak, and continued on beyond.

She darted out into the hall and ducked into an empty room. The closet door was closed. She had to ease it open and it squeaked. Right on the other side was a throaty chuckle and the door banged open.

Linda shrieked and ran, and Mitch laughed. She was halfway down the hall when he caught her. She struggled in a token way, they were both laughing, and he scooped her up to carry her to his room. He paused at the doorway to say, "There are formal meanings to a man carrying his captive woman over his threshold. Pay attention."

And he took her to his bed. He forgot all about the sleeping bag. He laid her in the middle of the bed and told her not to move. Then he lay next to her and toyed with her and played and teased the way he'd dreamed. He took her and moved deliciously but then he withdrew.

He lay beside her and tasted her and suckled. He allowed a finger to tickle her intimately in little swirls that made her writhe. His eyes became coals, gleaming in the subdued light, and their breaths screened the sounds in the old creaking house.

When she was frantic and moving restlessly in her inflamed passion, he finally joined with her and moved in her to take her to rapture. She curled and writhed as if on fire, and her tiny squeaks were of such need that each movement was exquisitely thrilling.

His renewed hunger rushed to match hers. He panted as he led her on, building the tension in her to fever pitch, to the incredible pause before the starburst explosion of the pent-up, erotic release. Then came the freefall, the spiraling slowly back downward in the falls of the after-shocks.

They lay spent for a long, long time. The only movement had been when he'd dragged his chest over a bit and lay half off her to one side, but they were still coupled.

He finally dragged himself free, to her murmured protests, went to the bathroom and came back to climb back into his bed to his hard-won treasure. He kissed her chastely, pulled the sheet up over them, and they went to sleep.

He wakened in the night and found her there. It was a dream come true and one he could not resist. He caressed her stealthily, thrilling to the feeling of tasting forbidden fruit. As his passion mounted and he became bolder, she murmured in her sleep.

Even that thrilled him, like seeing her going up the stairs naked, and the actuality of finding and capturing her as he had last night. His hands searched more boldly, relishing her under them, squeezing and kneading. Searching her out. Playing with her. Turning her and moving over her.

"What are you doing?" she asked groggily.

"Guess."

"Ah-hah!"

And he did. With great pleasure. She was still moist from his last invasion, so he slid easily into her sheath, and he made love to her the way he wanted, the way he'd dreamed. He just went ahead and took great delight in her, with no hesitation.

Languidly, she allowed that. He was intent, concentrated, greedy. And he reached his climax with delicious release, shuddering and almost convulsing, his voice hoarse with his heavy breathing.

Then he propped himself on his elbows until he'd recovered enough to roll away from her. He patted her arm and said, "By golly. Umm-ummph."

She laughed a bell tinkle of sound. She was amused. And that charmed Mitch. That she would tolerate his selfish taking. She was truly a remarkable woman.

He dragged himself off to the bathroom to discard the protection, then came back to climb into bed, take her into his arms and go instantly back to sleep. Linda was truly amused. He was rather like a train, through the station in no time at all.

It was morning when they wakened the next time. He was watching her soberly. "You're a miracle."

"That's a nice attitude. I should encourage you thinking that, but I'm just a woman."

"You do tend to be a tad literal, but you have such humor. You can tease, and that last time you were very kind to a needy bed partner. Thank you."

She grinned. "I wasn't doing anything anyway." And he laughed. He relaxed back on the bed and just laughed in the most wonderful low chuckle. The sound of it filled her soul in such a strange way. He was a special man. "Do all women feel this way about their first lover?"

His head snapped around and he frowned, "Just what do you mean about 'first' lover."

"You have to know I've never had anyone else."

"You didn't 'had' me, we made love."

"That last time—"

He was emphatic. "That was love of another kind."

"Phooey. Any female body would have filled the bill."

"You can't know how much I dreamed of having you here with me. I haven't had a good night's sleep since I first laid eyes on you. I've never had that trouble before in all my life."

"I enjoyed it."

"I didn't wait for you."

"It was very nice. I liked having you want me that way, and I didn't mind you going ahead."

"You are the nicest thing that's ever happened to me. You're a dream."

She stretched. She'd never realized a stretch was tantalizingly sexual, but she found out that it was.

That morning they had just entered the kitchen when the cat yowled to get inside. He'd been out all night and was not only hungry but exhausted. After his breakfast, he went into the living room, flopped down on the sofa and slept instantly.

Mitch stood with an arm around Linda looking at the cat, and he told her, "I know exactly how he feels."

"Do you have any guests scheduled to arrive?"

"Nope."

"Oh." And she smiled.

"You're here all alone with the lusty innkeeper, with no one to protect your virtue."

"Too late."

"You may be a little literal, but you make up for that in sassiness."

She sassed, "I've never been sassy in all my life."

"Then you're making unusual headway. Just because you have me wrapped around your little finger, you must think you're something."

"I have a strong feeling I can get your attention any time I take off my clothes."

He put back his head and laughed before he promised, "Even with them on."

"How could this have happened so fast?"

"Fast? It's taken me five whole days and five terrible nights to get you into my bed."

"And you're supposed to be shy. Lee said that the first evening when I arrived. Five days is hardly the work of a shy man."

"I am shy. It was you. You seduced me. I warned you about sashaying over to the sofa that way, but you just went right ahead and slinked right on over and— After that, it's all a blur. Did I fight at all?"

"Not that I recall."

"My mother would be so disappointed in me. I should have at least made a token struggle to preserve my virtue."

She gave him a patient smile and unfairly inquired, "How come you had protection for me?"

"Uh... Uh... Let's see. Why did I have protection? That's the question, isn't it? Just give me a minute. I know there's a plausible reason here, somewhere, I just have to think of it."

And she laughed.

He kissed her a couple of times, but when his breathing changed, she squirmed away and told him to behave. That shocked him, that she would think he would misbehave. She chortled.

"I've never heard anyone chortle before this very day. How'd you know how to do that? Have other men kissed you that way?"

"No. And I've never even sat on a sofa with another man."

"How about cars? You a car necker?"

She admitted, "A couple of cars."

"Station wagons?"

"No. They're like sofas. A smart woman avoids station wagons and sofas."

"How about men? Do smart women avoid men?"

"Not at all. Men are fun to be around. But a woman doesn't tempt a man. She doesn't kiss him overly much or allow him to fool around."

"What about me? You going to let me go on fooling around with you?"

"Probably."

"Holy mackerel. Don't just come right out and say 'probably' that way. You want to cripple me?"

"You couldn't possibly be interested after last night and this morning."

"Don't tempt fate."

"Then I should say, 'No'?"

"Well, no. But you ought to hesitate and pretend I have to work at it a little more. To know you're so willing tantalizes me excruciatingly."

"Bosh."

He laughed. "I have to get to work on this house, if it's going to be ready in time."

"In time? You've said that before. When are your next guests due?"

"I haven't any more. None with reservations."

"Do you need money? I can give you what I owe you so far."

"No. We have to talk about that, pretty soon now. You really didn't get full treatment. You should have had a full set of furniture, so the bill won't be hardly nothing at all and maybe not even that."

"You can't run a business that way," she admonished. Then she added, "I haven't anything to do today. I'm just supposed to be available in case someone at Stewart's has to call me. By now, they know how to find and solve their own problems. But sometimes there's a potential genius who can really gum up the works. As long as I can hear the phone, I can help you do whatever you want, except move furniture upstairs."

"Well, darn. I thought we might stock the attic. I love watching you go upstairs."

"You have a walking-upstairs fetish?"

"Yeah, I guess I must. You move so pretty. I just die when I see you climb the stairs."

"That could be trying, if that's all you'd want from me."

"Oh, no. There's a couple of other things. Like getting into my bed and being ready for me. And the list could expand, with kissing and hugging and stuff like that."

"Make a list and I'll check it out."

"I'm not a writer, I'm a demonstrator. I just found that out last night. So I'll have to show you all the things I like and let you agree."

"You are implying that I may not disagree, that I can only agree?"

"That's about the size of it."

And again she laughed that man-maddening laugh.

He had to have a kiss, and she did allow one, but then she pried his hands away so that she stood free. "I have to call and tell Bob Stewart that I have a copy of their tape. It could be important if anyone's loused up."

"The phone call is free."

"That's exciting." She was being droll.

"And we can trade privileges. I can show you what you can trade when you tell me what you need." He licked his lips and looked politely attentive.

"I'll just use the phone."

And he said, "Well, darn. That's the only thing around here today that you can do for free."

Nine

In the late morning, still on that Monday, Linda called Bob Stewart at his store and said, "This is Linda Parsons. I know it's cheating for me to contact you. I should just wait, but I need to tell you that I made a copy of the payroll tape on Friday."

There was an odd pause. Then Bob said, "Did you, now. That was thoughtful." He paused again before he asked almost tersely, "Where is the tape?"

"Here, in my room."

"Good. Keep it for now, will you? We're getting along very well. There's no need for you to come over at all," he said firmly. Then he added, "Linda, since you aren't at the original bed-and-breakfast, where are you?"

"At the bed-and-breakfast. It's at 1201 Premont with a 'P' not an 'F.' Some of the brochures were wrong."

There was yet another pause and Bob said, "I'll be in touch."

As she hung up, Linda frowned and wondered what Bob had meant about her not being at the *original* bed-and-breakfast? She'd been here all along.

She went up the stairs and down the hall to where Mitch was installing the upstairs hot-water heater. "How come you're only putting that in now? I could have had a hot shower any time. This will be marvelous."

"We'll take a shower right after lunch."

"We?" She was really shocked by the idea and even more so when she realized her body's reaction was thrills of excitement.

Mitch's green eyes showed fiery yellow lights. "We," he confirmed.

She held tools for him and handed them to him as he asked for them and she was kissed, each time, for being such a help. It only took him about twice as long as usual to get the heater put in and connected up.

Then Helen Nelson, from Stewart's, called and said, "You should know how right you were about making a copy and taking it offsite. We lost our entire payroll tape over the weekend. Something happened and it's blank. We don't have a backup. I thought Bob was going to copy it, and he thought I had done it."

Linda laughed.

Mrs. Nelson was stiff with indignation. "It's not funny. That will delay the payroll for over a month! It will inconvenience every one of us."

"I am sorry. I didn't mean to offend you, but you need not worry at all. I saw that Bob hadn't copied the tape on Friday after work, so I made one and brought it here. Bob must be underlining the lesson of being careful. I called him a while ago and told him I had a copy."

"You made a copy and have it with you?"

"Yes," Linda admitted carefully. "He told me to keep it here."

"When was this?" Mrs. Nelson asked.

"About an hour ago."

Mrs. Nelson was silent a minute, then she said, "Don't give the tape to anyone. I'll call you back in a little while."

"All right."

Linda went back to Mitch and told him about the two conversations. That made alarm bells soundlessly boom all through his body. "Something's going on."

"I don't know. It could be that Bob's trying to impress the staff with how important it is to copy and to get a copy offsite."

"Don't leave the house."

"Leave?" She was startled. "I really don't have to go anywhere. Mrs. Nelson is going to call me back in a little while."

"I don't want you to answer the door. Understand? I'll take care of things. Get the tape and give it to me."

"Bob said—"

"What he says makes no difference. I want you to give me the tape. I'll be responsible for it."

She stood before him, not as big as he, nor as wide as he but equal to him. Her glance weighed him and she nodded. "I trust you."

He had never known such a thrill as that. It was different from the sexual thrill of her. It was different from anything he'd ever experienced. He was an honest man, he expected trust, but she really didn't know him very well. She was an indecipherable woman and she had put her trust in his hands. It touched him that she would do that, say it in just that way. He told her, "Thank you."

"I'm not sure I'm doing you a favor. I could get you in lots of trouble. I probably should call Dallas and ask what they would have me do under these circumstances. It would be very awkward not to give it to Bob, he's the head of the company."

"What did he tell you to do with it?"

"To keep it here."

"We'll do that. Get it for me, now, and I'll put it somewhere safe."

"Where?"

"Somewhere. It's best that you don't know."

"I don't believe there's any problem. Mrs. Nelson is hyper because someone shredded the payroll some months ago and there was the month's delay on salaries and wages for the whole outfit. It was a real annoyance, and Bob's father had a fit. Literally. He is incapacitated. He must be a real rotten man with a terrible temper. They're all afraid he'll get well and take control again."

"Interesting. The payroll deal happened before? When?"

"I don't know. Apparently within the year. I didn't inquire into that. It was some time after the father brought Jim to work there. Jim's a strange man. Wavers between being abrasive and being very nice."

"So Jim was nice to you. What's he like?"

"You met both Jim and Bob. They came by here. You told them that I wasn't registered here."

"Honey, neither man came by here. They went somewhere else. I don't know them. But neither knows exactly where you are, either. That's to the good."

Linda shook her head. "I told Bob. He thought the bed-and-breakfast was on Fremont Avenue. I explained where I am and about the brochure being misprinted."

Mitch looked blankly patient. "So you told him exactly how to find you?"

"Just the correct address."

"I see." He chewed on his lower lip as he watched her, then he went downstairs to the front door and opened it, whistled shrilly and yelled, "Gato! Get in here!"

He called only once and waited. Pretty soon the black cat came bounding over the unkempt lawn and up the stairs with exquisite grace, stopped and walked in with an inquiring meow. Mitch squatted down and petted the cat, tilting its head up so that they had eye contact, then Mitch said, "Guard." And he indicated Linda.

Linda burst out laughing. The cat sat down and watched her with interest. Mitch stood up and put his hands on his hips in the patient way males have when they must endure.

Her laughter was all that rang in the house. She tried to control it, but it bubbled forth in amused delight. "Guard? That cat? He has no interest in anything but that calico outside, his food and a place to sleep. And you expect that cat to guard me? You are hilarious. I had thought you were worried about this tape incident. It has potential for being very sticky, but I realize you've been joshing me. I am a little literal, but I can recognize this ridiculous farce as the humor you intend. You were trying to lead me into believing this was really serious. But you went too far. That cat! To *guard* me? Mitch, this is priceless. You are so funny. That little cat. He *is* big for a cat, but as a guard cat? Oh, Mitch.'' And laughter took her.

She jiggled when she laughed, so he didn't stop her or explain. He just waited until she'd quieted and stood with laughter still spilling from her blue eyes. She was beautiful. Wonderful. She had such a nice laugh. It was just as well that she thought he was playing a game.

''So, let me keep the tape.''

Obediently, she went to fetch it and handed it to him. ''Here is the Grail. Do you take it to Camelot, Sir Knight?''

''Something like that. Count to a hundred. Close your eyes and turn to the wall. Then count.''

Where could he hide a tape in that house? She already knew all the hiding places. Indulgently she turned to the wall, covered her eyes and began to count. ''One, two, three...''

After thirty-five she allowed her hands to slide from her face and she looked around, counting more slowly, listening. She could hear nothing. Had he left the house? Still counting, she decided he'd gone outside and put it in his car. That low, snarling, dangerous-looking car. A good hiding place. The machine was intimidating. Not too many people would approach it. It looked as if it might turn around and bite like a mean horse.

Her fancy was still expanding on that car when Mitch suddenly appeared in the hall, as if he'd just been beamed aboard from *Star Trek*'s *Enterprise*. She jumped with startled surprise, and he asked, "Why aren't your eyes covered?"

"I was listening."

"You listen with your eyes?"

"Of course. When people listen very intently, they move their eyes. Notice."

"Why were you listening?"

She smiled the faintest little bit and replied, "So I didn't skip any of the numbers."

He grinned at her and said, "You're very sassy. Do you know what happens to sassy women?"

"I get to fix lunch?"

"Not right away."

He proved that the new hot-water heater worked for the shower. But as he soaped her down, he lost track of the water demonstration and became very involved in anatomy. He was astounded by how different she was and he showed her the oddities of her peculiarly shaped and functioning body. He questioned how various things worked. And he had to experiment and taste in order to fully understand.

He dried her carefully and scrubbed his own body dry, then he carried her into his room for further investigation. Without ever moving from the bed, he drove her right up the wall. And he loved it. He had her on her ear, she was so frantic. And he toyed with her.

He lounged on the bed, braced on one elbow, so masculine, so confident in his maleness, so pleased with her. He allowed her to touch him, to feel the difference of his hair-textured chest and arms and that on his legs. He would twitch and purr and murmur. He let her feel the fullness of him, and he encouraged her to satisfy her curiosity.

She was really getting bold. She tasted his lips, and found his flat nipples in the swirl of his chest hair. Then she had to explore his hairy navel and poke her tongue inside. She explored other places, too, touching and smoothing and feeling, licking and using her fingers and palms.

It was interesting to see the difference from the lounging man to the riveted one. She didn't allow him to touch in turn. She made him lie flat on his back and clasp his hands on top of his head. Then she was free to do as she chose without being interrupted.

His smile was different, too, hot and chewed. His eyes were avidly watching her, unless he had to close them as he groaned or took a sharp breath. Watching him, she pretended her finger was a flea, and it scurried in little, insidious trackings through the hair of his body. "Does that tickle?"

Hoarsely he said, "No."

But she leaned back and laughed. Then she had to make him put his hands back on top of his head and lie back down.

There's a limit to what any man can endure, and that limit did come. And he curled up and took control of his protesting lover. She commanded that he lie back down, that she wasn't through with him yet.

"Oh, yes."

Then he continued in his own way. And their pleasure was intense. They made leisurely, experimental love—and the phone rang. Naturally.

After the fifteenth ring, Mitch said something rude and got up from the bed, stalked magnificently naked out into the hall and down to the reading room at the top of the stairs, to the phone. "Yes?"

And Nick's voice said, "What's going on? I had a call *here* about not having my bed-and-breakfast registered and inspected. I have to show up for a hearing. Your little farce is getting out of hand."

"I'll take care of it."

"How?" Nick wanted to know.

"I'll call my uncle."

"Why are you acting so testy? It's *my* neighbors who are complaining."

"It's probably Molly who brought over glue pies and was trying to get into my pants," Mitch suggested nastily.

"How shocking."

"So is Molly."

"A real horror?" Nick was shocked.

"No. Just too pushy."

"And then there's Linda."

"Careful," Mitch warned.

"That bad, huh."

"She's a gem."

"Good," Nick said in satisfaction.

"How's the little mother and my godchild?"

"Sleepy."

"And the new papa?"

"I haven't touched ground since."

"He's a fine boy."

"Isn't he, though. You ought to get married and have some."

Mitch laughed. "Some?"

"Kids."

"All new fathers feel that way, once it's over. I believe I can recall a very worried, nervous man not twenty-four hours ago."

"God. What a sweat."

Mitch heard the tremor in Nick's voice and knew Nick felt as if he'd been pulled through a knothole.

Nick asked, "Are you coming up to see us?"

"Will it be too much?"

"No. Little Mitch asked about you just a couple of minutes ago. He said he needed another look at you before the christening. He wants to pass on you as godfather."

"His daddy promised me the job, the kid doesn't have any input at all. Tell him the deal's closed. *Tell me about Bob Stewart.*"

"What do you want to know?"

"Is he dangerous?"

There was a startled pause. "I don't *think* so, but his dad's a madman. Always was. Everybody at the warehouse was relieved when he went nuts earlier this year. He had a real *fit!* Something happened at the business that ticked him off. He went out of control. It must have been something to see. But the old man was always that way. In control, but with a fine edge. Bob's never been that way, that we know. The old man was abusive. But I believe it was only verbal. Derision. Put-downs. That sort of thing."

"Humiliating."

"Right. The old man's a bully. Everything was his way. Bob had a hard time of it, but he didn't have enough strength to tell the old man to go to hell and then leave the business. Tell you what, Bob's coming up about eight-thirty tonight, why don't you come up just a bit after that and you can look him over?"

"Good. I'll do that."

"Did you get the upstairs hot-water heater connected?"

Mitch turned to look down the hall toward his room, and Linda was standing there in the doorway to the back hall, naked, with something flimsy held to her chest that slid down to cover her body just barely enough. With her love-tousled hair and big blue eyes, she was a man's dream.

"Did you?" Nick asked.

"Yes."

"Well, see you tonight. Could you bring me a couple of pairs of jeans? They're hanging on the left side of our closet."

"No problem."

"I don't know how I forgot jeans when I packed to come here, but I have eight shirts and only the jeans I'm standing in."

"Yeah." Mitch wasn't paying much attention to Nick.

"And get everything done so I can rest when I get home. This being a father wears a man out."

"Yes."

"At least get all the doorknobs on the doors. I hate doing that."

"Doorknobs."

"You've surely done a great job on our house. You get a permanent room there for the rest of your life. Who're you slated to do next?"

Mitch smiled a very slow, dangerous smile at Linda and said, "I'll let you know."

"Well, see you tonight."

"Fine." He hung up very carefully, his focus never leaving Linda's stare. And in a low, growly voice, he asked her, "What are you doing out of my bed?"

And the humor crept into those blue eyes. She tilted her chin up, just a little but she didn't reply.

Mitch walked over to her in a way that melted her bones, and she had to lean back against the door-jamb. The hand holding her silk slip to her chest faltered and the garment slipped a little.

He took the slip and put it to his face, breathing in her perfume. Then he put it over his shoulder, pulled her close to him and kissed her.

It was no great surprise when he lifted her over his shoulder and carried her back to his room. He slid her onto the bed and stood over her, feasting his eyes on her. Then he crawled onto the bed, onto her, and he made wild and passionate love to her.

Lunch was a little late. And their naps shot most of the afternoon. Mitch managed to get the doorknobs on all the inner doors, but he made Linda go off somewhere else to read. Then he had to check on her to be sure she was all right. She laughed at him.

At supper she inquired, "Aren't you going to get the rest of the bedrooms papered? You haven't done much today at all. When is your opening?"

He wondered when he would have to tell her that he'd lied to her about the house being a bed-and-breakfast. And worse: how would she take it? She'd said liars were the worst thing she knew. He needed a few more days. When Nick brought Lee and the baby home in a couple of days, then would be the time to tell Linda the truth. He'd be through with the Smiths' house, and he could go back to Dallas with Linda.

There he would convince her to move back to Waco, and he could finish the other houses he had lined up to remodel and refurbish. She could stay with him and after those were finished, he'd take her back out west near Big Spring where they belonged.

"Are you a die-hard city girl?"

"Dallas." That said it all.

"You need to see West Texas."

"What all's out there?"

"Beautiful land, bushes, trees, mountains, canyons that are wonderful, the best people in all the world, and a peace you have to know."

She smiled slyly. "Nothing to do?"

He laughed. "You'd be surprised."

"I don't think so. I've known you for six days."

"The best days in all my life. I have to go to the hospital tonight and take some things to Nick. Only family can go up now. I'm listed as a close relative." Then in the dictatorial way of men, he directed her: "I want you to stay inside, lock the door, and don't answer either the phone or the door. Understand?"

"Okay."

He looked at her soberly. Then he got up and went to her chair to lift her up and hug her. "I didn't mean to sound so rough. I really mean, 'Will you, please?' but it comes out like a directive." He thought about that and admitted, "Actually, I mean it as a directive. You'd think I could get the point across without being so blunt, but I need you to understand. Don't answer the phone, or the door, and stay inside. Please."

"Okay!" Her reply wasn't quite so accepting.

He heard that and was alarmed, so he took a little time. He cupped a gentle, large hand on her shoulder and he shook it just a little as he said, "Humor me."

She gave him a droll look and retorted, "All I've done in the last couple of days is humor you."

His eyes glinted in response, but he coaxed, "You sound so put-upon."

She snorted.

"Who was that woman who was wiggling and screeching and begging? She wasn't 'humoring' me."

Linda grinned, then laughed.

Mitch asked softly, "Please, do this for me."

"You feel uneasy about this tape?"

"I don't exactly know why. It's just a feeling. I'm going to meet Bob Stewart tonight at the hospital. I want to check him out. He makes me nervous."

"Do that. I'll be fine here. I have the Killer Cat to guard me." She couldn't prevent a grin. That was so ridiculous.

"Don't underestimate Gato."

"He doesn't even wear a sword." She was derisive.

"He has them on all his toes."

"True. But—"

"Stay inside, don't answer the phone or the door. Okay?"

"Yes." She hissed the word with impatience.

So just before light, Mitch gathered a couple of pairs of jeans from the front corner bedroom the Smiths had taken over, and he cautioned Linda only about forty more times.

She became really impatient with him and said, "Go on!"

"I'll be back as soon as I can."

Becoming a shade irritated, Linda retorted, "I thought tonight was your night on the town."

"Don't get sassy." He kissed her. Then he hugged her very tightly and held her that way. "I'm in love with you."

"That isn't possible."

"You're in a disbelieving mood right now. Forget about my loving you and just concentrate on stay-ing—"

"Inside. Don't answer the phone or the door."

"Good. You're slow but you can learn." And he went out the door quickly and closed it.

She opened it for a final verbal shot, but he whipped around to glare at her. "I *told* you—"

She slammed the door.

Mitch drove, intently concentrated. He was antsy, and the unease got worse as he got farther from Linda. Maybe he ought to go back. Contrary as she was, she would obey. She trusted him. She'd said so. What if she had no choice? What if someone wanted that tape for a very serious reason that wasn't lawful? How could a payroll tape be unlawful? If the money was being stolen. If the foul-up was deliberate so that the money could be temporarily funneled into something else.

Like what? Like gambling? Like the stockmarket? Riding the ups and downs for a month could cost a fortune. How many shares could the payroll buy? With a hundred employees who made a minimum of a thousand a month, that would mean at least a hundred thousand dollars.

Who would do it? And what would they do to get that tape to protect the foul-up? This could well be deliberate. Was it Bob? Why had he told Linda to just keep the tape? Well, they wouldn't get it. He had it in the car, strapped under the top of the recess in the trunk.

What if someone did go to the fake bed-and-breakfast and confronted Linda and couldn't find the tape? What might he do to Linda?

Mitch ran into the hospital and hurried to the maternity floor. He washed his hands and donned the protective gown and washed his hands a second time in the disappearing foam.

Nick said, "Well, Mitch, here you are."

"Yeah."

"Thanks for bringing the jeans. This is Bob Stewart. He's an old acquaintance. Bob, this is Mitchell Roads."

Bob said, "Hi. How did you escape being called Dusty or something?"

"I'm not sure. Linda told me about the tape."

"She still has it?" Bob was intense.

"I want to know what's going on."

Nick said to Bob, "Mitch's okay."

"My father is a little off center. He's done this before. And he takes the money to Las Vegas for a month and gambles. He's won both times. This is too much. It's wrong. It inconveniences the workers. Helen and I figured with the computer system we'd have it stopped, but damned if he didn't get to the tapes. Two of them."

"You had an offsite one?"

"Yes. How he found out where it was is something we'll have to know. He isn't reliable."

"Can he know about the third tape?"

Bob admitted, "I don't know. He's been to the bed-and-breakfast on Fremont. I called and asked. He went there personally about six this evening."

"I'll call Linda. I have to get back to her."

But of course, Linda didn't answer the phone.

* * *

She was reading in her room and listening to the phone ringing and ringing. But after it finally stopped, it began again.

It was about twenty minutes later, and the phone had been silent for at least five minutes, when the cat came into the room. It arched its back and hissed outward toward the hall.

That raised all the fine, little hairs on Linda's back.

The cat looked at her, then turned away again and hissed toward the hall. Then it went to the closet door and looked at Linda.

They stared at each other, then the cat looked back at the hall, again back to Linda, its pupils wide, and it put one paw on the closet door.

As quietly as possible, Linda turned off the light, slid off the bed and carefully went to the closet door. She opened it slowly, carefully, and she and the cat went inside. It was very dark. Linda was afraid of the dark.

Ten

A little claustrophobic on top of everything else, Linda stood in the closet with the cat and thought, What am I doing in here? This dumb cat wants an adventure in the house, and just because I heard Mitch tell the cat to "guard" me, I accept that as real? Linda, she said to herself, you are over the edge of all good reason.

She moved to leave the closet, and the cat hissed.

She was the prisoner of a mad cat? What if that got into the papers? Demented woman found prisoner of cat five-fifty-sevenths of her size.

She'd lose her job. They would say, "Miss Parsons, we are sorry but we shall have to release you from your position. It isn't that you allowed a cat to take you prisoner. No, no. It's because we're top-heavy in the executive branch of our operation, and Mr. Thornton has a family. You understand."

One can only allow oneself to be a victim. One takes charge of one's life. Linda left the closet and was headed across the room to the hall, when Gato dashed ahead of her and on out into the hall.

With her imagination, she "saw" the cat standing on his hind legs with his back braced against the front door to prevent her opening it. A cat only five-fifty-sevenths of her weight meant that she was bigger than the damned cat.

With determination, she marched to the door of her room, opened it wider and went out into the hall.

And she heard a sound.

She froze, listening. The silence popped in her ears. It was very eerie. She was so sensitized that it was a wonder she wasn't picking up radio stations.

A board creaked, and she was electrified. She probably glowed. She was being ridiculous. Being the prisoner of a determined cat was one thing, but being the victim of her imagination was outrag—

There was another sound. It was a sound caused by someone moving very silently. There was someone in the house who didn't want anyone else to know he was there.

He? It could be Molly, snooping.

"Damn!" a male voice hissed in the stairwell.

Who?

Quietly, quietly, she edged to the end of the hall to the reading room at the top of the stairs. She could still run if he came up those stairs. She needed to know her adversary.

The house was very still. A stair creaked, and Linda began to shiver. But she had to see.

Outside it was darker. The street lights cast shadows in the lightless interior. Linda could see the darker blur of Gato at the top of the stairs.

The man came to the landing. He was bulky. It wasn't Mitch. Until then she'd thought it might be Mitch. Good heavens. But she really didn't know.

As the man started up the steps from the landing and Linda pulled back, planning her path of flight, Gato launched himself with a snarling ferocity and hit the man on the head.

The man hoarsely screamed and struck out at his attacker before falling down several steps.

Linda fled. She dived into her room and into the closet, through it to the next room and down through the weaving hide-and-seek route of the second floor to the back stair, then down the stair to the maze of the storage rooms. There she could endlessly hide and elude anyone without ever having to expose an inch of herself.

She began to understand mice. She shivered with unspent energy, restless with inactivity. She wanted to run. Anything could have set her off.

Gato came. He made the tiniest warning sound, then he was there. He'd saved her. She put her hand out gratefully, and discovered he was wet. Wet? It was blood. He'd been hurt.

She made the slightest sound of sympathy and lifted the cat onto her lap, against her chest, holding it with great, tender sympathy.

Gato gave the briefest purr, then stiffened and wiggled to be released. She let him go.

She heard the man upstairs. He thought he was alone but for the cat, and now he made no pretense of stealth. He was ransacking the upstairs.

Linda kept an ear on the prowler's progress, went to the phone in the kitchen and called 911.

It was busy.

She disconnected with the button and counted to ten, dialed again, and it was busy. That happened a frustrating two times more, then a calm, *loud* voice said, "Police."

In a hoarse whisper, Linda said, "There's a man upstairs, a burglar, 1201 Premont, '*P*' as in Peter. He hurt the cat."

"1201 Premont. Where are you?"

"Downstairs. I'll be in the storage area behind the kitchen. Hurry." And she hung up and went back to the maze, and Gato growled at her for leaving.

She heard the car. She heard the thud of feet on the porch, and she was amazed the police were that quick. There must have been a squad ca—

The front door was thrown back against the wall. "Linda!" came Mitch's roar.

"Look out!" she screamed. "He's upstairs."

"Who?"

"I don't know. He hurt Gato."

"Linda? Are you all right?"

It was a voice she didn't recognize. The police, probably. "Yes."

Then that same voice called, "Dad?"

Upstairs was silence.

Dad? Who was with Mitch whose father was upstairs tearing up the place?

But then the sirens came in blurps out on the street, with flashing lights and there were thundering footsteps on the porch and around the house on the ground and on the drive. And there was a lot of thudding and exclamations and that same strange voice saying versions of "Dad!" any number of times. It all made Linda a little panicked.

Gato came back to her and leaned against her shin. She picked him up very carefully, knowing that he bled. She murmured to him, apologizing for thinking him anything but brilliantly brave. The cat purred to soothe her, but he was very alert and watching. Linda was strung on jerky strings.

Mitch came. He was wild. Lights came on. He tore open doors, yelling her name, and he found her. The lights blinded her.

He saw the blood, and his heart almost stopped. He whispered, "Linda. You're hurt."

She babbled, "No, no, no. It's Gato. He really *is* a guard cat. He saved my neck. He's hurt."

All was chaos but for the police who just calmly went about their business. The neighbors came saying this was what happened when strangers came into a neighborhood and tried to start a business that was illegal and brought questionable people into the neighborhood.

That caught the attention of the police. Mitch had to leave Linda standing against the porch wall, still holding the bloody cat, while he and Bob Stewart explained everything—out of her hearing—about the tape. The neighbors listened, fascinated, and the police were stoic.

Then Mitch explained to two of the more militant neighbors about the sham bed-and-breakfast at that address, and why. And Bob Stewart took his father away in one of the police cars.

Linda watched that. What on earth?

Then Mitch went out to the curb and talked to some of the other neighbors, and there was laughter. Linda frowned, wondering what could be funny in such a grim situation?

She went down the steps and approached amid a lot of attention directed to her. Amused attention. It made her bristle. She said sternly, "The cat flung himself at the intruder, and he was hurt. He needs help."

Cordially the neighbors gave the name of the nearest vet. One volunteered, "I'll call ahead, so the vet will be there." Another said to Mitch, "Go on, we'll keep an eye on the place for you."

Mitch put Linda and Gato into his car. He leaned in and looked at her. "You're sure you're all right?"

"Yes."

He went around the car and got inside to drive, and he put his hand on her shoulder all the way there. He asked three more times, "You are okay?" And she said "Yes" each time. Oddly, other than those words, neither spoke. Apparently it was enough just to know everything was all right for them, and they weren't ready to explore and discuss what had been so terribly wrong with Mr. Stewart.

At the veterinarian's office, Gato was awful. He strutted. He was arrogant. He demanded special treatment. They gave it.

The cat had a split lip, a torn ear, a closed eye and bruises. The vet tilted the cat's head back and dropped a pain pill down his throat. Then he put healing ointment in the eye. "When the excitement's over, he's going to hurt. This isn't his first brush with disaster. He has ridges and bumps all over him."

The vet put the cat into a hold, stitched the ear, and painted it with an antibiotic. By then the cat was really out of it, and the vet put in three perfect stitches on his lip. He also gave the cat his shots.

Since the anesthetic was so exact, Gato was already coming out of it and acted rather groggily drunk.

"The stitches will dissolve, don't worry about them. He'll feel rotten for a couple of days, but he's used to that and won't complain. He probably won't eat. He's used to that, too. Leave him alone. See to it he has water. If he goes longer than two days without drinking, bring him back for an I.V."

The bill came to just under a hundred dollars.

Linda insisted on paying, and then discovered she didn't have her purse.

Mitch told her, "I have to pay, he's my cat."

"But he saved my life."

"Then you'll have to stay with me and share him. I know good and well that your apartment house won't accept animals."

"You're right."

"You'll stay?"

"I can't have pets."

The vet smiled and left the room without ever getting back their attention.

Mitch asked again, "You are all right?"

"I did exactly as you told me. So did Gato." She looked at Mitch. "I apologize for laughing when you told Gato to guard me. I thought you were being ridiculous."

"I know."

"I am sorry. How did you know he would protect me?"

"He's a very smart cat. I just hope he sticks around and doesn't go off adventuring again."

"I was afraid—"

"I was spitless, with you alone and only a little cat to help you."

"—when you came up on the porch. I thought you might be killed. That man was tearing up the whole upstairs. He was Bob's *father*? Was *he* after the tape?"

The assistant came in and said, "Are you ready yet?"

They were supposed to leave. They said "Yes," and Linda picked up the cat.

The assistant gave Mitch a paper cloth. "You might want this on the way home. He could throw up. He's been through a lot and he might be a little upset."

Mitch carefully put the cat in the paper wrap and gave him to Linda. Then he paid their bill and bought a litter box and filler, so Gato wouldn't need to go out. They drove back to Premont Street slowly, taking care not to unsettle the woozy cat.

At the house they made a nest in a recessed place in one storeroom, and left the hero there with a bowl of water.

They finally went upstairs and viewed the mess. Linda's room was really a shambles. One lamp was broken, but the rest of it was just chaos. Nothing was shredded, just brutally searched and flung about.

Linda didn't want to change into any of her own clothes, which had been handled so roughly, so they closed the door and left the room untouched. They could tackle it the next day. They looked throughout the upstairs. Stewart had only begun on the Smiths' room. That straightening, too, the lovers left for the next day.

Mitch fetched a big shirt and some jeans for Linda. She took off the blood-stained clothes and put them to soak, then she showered and changed into Mitch's clothes. He got her a tie to use as a belt to keep the pants on. And he turned up the legs of the jeans, and he was pleased to have his clothes on her, for now.

They went downstairs and set a minimal scrap fire in the fireplace, brought in two glasses and a bottle of wine; and finally, they talked about it all.

Mitch told Linda, "Stewart is Bob's adopted father. Jim is the real son and illegitimate. Mr. Stewart brought Jim into the business without telling Bob the truth, and Bob thought his father didn't have any faith in his adopted son's business ability.

"Jim is equally competent, but inherited his father's abrasiveness, and Bob's fought back. The half brothers discussed the entire problem. They finally understood it was their father who was causing all the disruptions. At first they had suspected each other. Their father had been found to have shredded the second lost payroll, and being found out had caused the father's temper fit. He had shredded the payroll files because he wanted the delayed time to gamble with the money. Bob and Jim now have a clear understanding, and things will be different from now on."

"I'm glad. They're both nice men. How did he know the tape was here?"

"They aren't sure. They think maybe he had the office phone bugged."

"What a strange man."

"You're sure you're okay?"

The cat moved gingerly into the room, made the hearth with determination and lay down with a careful sigh, to sleep almost instantly.

Mitch and Linda looked at each other, then got up to fetch the clean rag rug, the water and the litter box and put them by the hearth. "I hope he doesn't expect to have all this stuff in the living room *all* the time." Mitch gave Linda a very sweet look.

"You're a pushover."

"Yeah. Does that make you feel all mushy for me? There you sit in my clothes, and I'm so envious of them I'm uncomfortable."

"I think your clothes are just like you, they're busy rubbing me in odd places."

"That's shocking, Miss Parsons."

"I was scared silly."

"My God, I didn't know what I was doing except that I had to get back to you. As soon as I got to the hospital, I knew I had to be back here. But I went ahead. Bob told me the whole story on the way here and my brain did listen, I did understand, but all I could think about was you."

"Did you phone?"

"Yes."

"When the phone just rang and rang and rang, I wondered if it was you."

"While it's good you are obedient, and I want you to go on that way, I— How many times did it ring?"

"At least twenty times."

"That one wasn't me."

She shivered.

He went to her and finally took her against him. "Linda. My God. Linda. I about died when we got to the house and there wasn't one light on."

She shivered again. It was simply reaction. Everything was okay now, but she'd lasted through a very interesting time and now she could react.

He held her and rubbed her body with his big, hard hands to warm her, then he groaned and crushed her to him. His voice shook as he said, "I was afraid to touch you. I had to be careful of you or I might have squeezed the breath out of you, I wanted to be sure you were all right. When I saw the blood on you, I just about died. I love you, Linda."

And she believed him. So she nodded in agreement. It had been a very emotional evening. She had been scared out of her wits and worried and now she knew she was in love with him in the forever way. It was all very unsettling.

She pushed gently against him and looked up to smile at him. There were big tears in her eyes, but her smile was so soft and sweet that he felt his own eyes prickle. He said, "You love me, don't you?" He was positive.

"It hasn't even been a week."

"I knew as soon as I saw you on the porch." Hold it, he cautioned himself. Careful. Don't tell yet.

"Since you really haven't gotten started in the bed-and-breakfast, why don't you sell this marvelous house, maybe to the Smiths? Come to Dallas with me. There're all kinds of building projects there. You can live with me."

"I'd like that very much."

"You will?" Her voice went up in excitement. "I know it will just kill you to give up this house. If you would do that for me, I would do anything you ask."

"Anything?"

"Yes. Ask."

"Marry me."

She blinked. After her offer, she really expected to be out of her clothes by this time. "Marry?"

"Yes."

"We ought to know each other a little longer."

"A whole week?" He acted surprised.

"How can we tell the kids we only knew each other a week?" She was aghast. "Think of the influence! A month. Six weeks would be better."

"I don't think I can last that long."

"You won't...you wouldn't...you don't want to—"

"Oh, yes. And I'm pleased, Miss Parsons, that you want, too."

She curled nicely—

And the phone rang.

He put Linda back from him and said seriously as he looked at her sternly, "We're not going to have a phone anywhere around." He got up and went into the library where he picked up the phone and said, "Yeah?"

"Well," Nick said with impatience, "what happened?"

With no punctuation or even spaces between the words, Mitch told his friend the bare bones. Then he added, "Tell Lee that her cat was a hero." Then he hung up.

Mitch came back to the sofa and smiled a salesman's smile. "Where were we?"

"Page ninety-three."

"That far along? Why are you still in my clothes?"

"Oops, sorry."

He was torn between wanting out of his own clothes and watching her disrobe with no distractions. He watched. She unbuttoned the shirt that had covered her so voluminously revealing only the smallness of her shoulders and giving only points of indications as to what lay beneath the cloth. She was revealed as fragile silk from a rough pod. Then she stood to undo his tie from around her waist and, with the zipper still closed, she slid the pants off her hips.

She stepped from the trousers, and he sucked in a quick breath. She surveyed him soberly. "How can I be naked and you still clothed?"

"Yes." He heaved to his feet and made short work of the problem.

His clothes covered his power. Revealed were the muscles that roiled under his tanned flesh, the hardness and breadth of him. Naked, she sat with her feet under her at one end of the sofa, one arm along the back of it, and she smiled as she avidly watched him.

Her interst made him shiver with desire and—

The phone rang.

"Ignore it," he snapped.

"They might worry." She got off the sofa, and he was treated to the sight of her walking nude into the library. She leaned over, and he watched the weight of her breasts shift as she lifted the phone to her ear and said, "Hello?"

Lee said in a rush, "You tell Mitch that cat is *his*! And when he's through there, at the house, he is to *take that cat with him*! I'm glad everything is okay. Goodbye."

Linda looked at the phone, then set it gently into the cradle. She turned toward Mitch and looked at him, waiting for her, standing by the sofa, magnificently naked.

"Who was it?" he asked intensely.

"Lee."

"What'd she say?" He was getting cautious.

"Gato is yours."

"Yeah?" Every shred of attention was riveted on her, trying to read her.

She walked back into the living room. "And...when you leave here...you are to take the cat with you."

"Oh."

She curled up on the end of the sofa, just as she had been when the phone rang. She lay one perfect arm along the back of the sofa as she lifted her eyes to Mitch. "Is there something you'd like to tell me?"

"No. I don't want to tell you one part of this, but I can tell you that I've loved you from the second I set eyes on you and I don't know why."

She drew her hand toward her along the back of the sofa and lay her cheek on it as she looked at him.

Mitch watched how her body shifted slightly and how one soft breast was pressed against the back of the sofa. His body loved looking at her. His tongue stayed silent.

"Lee said, 'when you leave here.' Where are you going?"

"To Dallas to be a kept man."

"They know about this?"

"No."

"Then how do they know you're going to Dallas with me?"

He smiled his nicest smile, trying to lead her from the course that conversation had taken. "So you admit you're going to keep me?"

"I make a good salary. To quote you, there's 'no problem'."

"You're going to lock me in a tower and use me for carnal purposes?" He grinned wickedly, again confident.

"On occasion." She gave him a heavy lidded look.

He thought he was past the crisis, and he put his hands under her armpits and slowly, slowly, with

awesome muscles, he lifted her up high above his
head, looking up at her.

She never took her gaze from his, and she hung
there delectably, temptingly helpless. He pulled his
hands closer above him so that her body came to his
face and open-mouthed, he kissed her stomach, then
he slid her very slowly down his hard body.

She opened her legs and caught him between her
thighs, and he held her there, their eyes almost level.
Since he looked down slightly, his green eyes were
somewhat screened, but her blue eyes were wide,
trusting... and questioning. He told her, "I've loved
you all along." He moved his arms so that they enclosed her, and he put her gently on her feet, still
holding her.

"Yes."

"I lied to you. This isn't a bed-and-breakfast. The
house belongs to the Smiths. When you came up on
the porch, I wanted to carry you to my den right then,
and defend my having you against all comers. The
next best thing was to tell you that you were expected
here and bluff it out."

"Yes."

"It was the only thing I could think to do. If I'd told
you the truth, I would have had a hard time getting to
know you well enough in the little time you would be
here. You would have thought me crude and pushy
and you would have gone out with Bob or Jim and you
wouldn't have given me another thought." His eyes
were very serious, his voice roughened. "So I had to
do what I did. I lied."

"Yes."

"I'd lie again, just the same way."

"Yes."

"And you forgive me?"

"Yes."

"You love me."

"Yes."

"Oh, Linda, I've sweated blood over that lie. When you told me you hated liars worse than anything, I thought my goose was cooked."

"No."

"And you really love me enough to put up with me?"

"I'll have to see. A man who lies has to be careful all the rest of his life or he gets it thrown in his face at awkward times. But if the woman loves the man, and understands and appreciates how smart he was to lie at a particular time, then she doesn't mind at *all*, but smiles and says how brilliantly he acted." She smiled up at him and added, "You were brilliant. I was completely convinced. I love you."

She almost unmanned him. He turned so tender and loving. He was holding her as if she was a precious, fragile wisp that might disappear if he breathed wrong. She laughed in her throat.

With an unsteady voice, he instructed, "I want you to walk up the stairs to my room. Please."

She considered that rather elaborately. She put her hands behind her back and clasped them there. She considered his direction, and she looked about as she decided. She went up on her toes and dropped back to her heels so that her breasts jiggled and shimmered.

He was mesmerized.

She turned away and then looked back, confident that she had his attention. She did. And she finally gave one exaggerated nod and said, "I'll do it," as if she'd agreed to the trek to the South Pole.

He accused, "You're a tease!"

"I?" She pointed to her bare breast.

"You *are*, and I've agreed to marry you and I'll spend my entire life being tortured like a fat cat. By jingo, I *knew* when I saw you that you'd be worth the trouble."

"Trouble." She tasted the word.

"And worry," he agreed. "A worthwhile pain. Git up them steps, woman."

She leaned forward and her breasts hung from her chest. "Say please."

Effortlessly he went down on his knees, his eyes glinting, and he growled threateningly, "Please."

She stretched, lifting her hair and allowing it to fall back as her hands went higher. With the stretch deliciously done, she relaxed, looked at Mitch and said, "Well, okay."

With terrific balance, he rose to his feet and waited.

She turned away, glanced back over her shoulder to see if he followed, and he did. She went to the bottom of the stairs and paused. "Now?"

He steadied, then said, "Now!" on an indrawn breath.

And she took her time. She went up the stairs with only the slightest enhancement to her movements. She looked back, her glance flirting just enough, and she paused several times. At the landing she waited while he came up those stairs seemingly in two bounds.

He sprawled on the window-seat's purple cushions and said, "Now will you go up those stairs?"

She had to make the decision. And she tortured him in doing that. She was astonished that she knew what to do. She'd never tried to tempt a man before. But she turned and posed and displayed her body to him.

And he watched, red-eyed.

She went up the stairs as she had before, and this time he followed with equal decorum. He didn't touch or pat or pinch. He watched.

Turning back now and then to observe him, she went ahead. And he followed. She went to his room and paused in the doorway, her head down to glance back from the sides of her eyes. Her smile was very faint, almost concealed.

"What you do to me should be outlawed for any other man. *I* can handle it."

"I would like to touch you."

"Go right ahead."

She went to him and put her hands on his hairy chest, smoothing his breasts and rubbing his nipples. He did that to her.

She lowered her hands to his stomach and followed the hair pattern lower to stroke the textured skin. He did that to her.

She taunted his excited interest and ran her hands down, then slowly back up his thighs. He groaned, picked her up and took her to his bed. There he tore open the packet with trembling fingers and rolled on the protection. Then he laid her down and took her.

The surge of passion was euphoric, and they stopped and panted, trying to breathe. He moved with care and tenderness that turned into hard and demanding thrusts. She met him, her hands pulling at him, her mouth open, her eyes closed. Then the thrusts shortened and quickened as they reached for the thrilling climax. They paused and convulsed with ecstasy. They floated, weightless, until they finally fell back, to lie in a tangle of sweat-filmed bodies. Replete. Exhausted.

After a while, he mumbled, "So, Miss Parsons, you like sex."

"Umm."

"And me? Do you like me?"

She lifted her arms and enclosed his head against her soft breasts. "I love you."

"It's just a good thing you do."

*   *   *   *   *

SILHOUETTE Desire™

COMING NEXT MONTH

#571 SLOW BURN—Mary Lynn Baxter
Lance O'Brien's kidnapping was over in a moment. Marnie Lee was
left to deal with the aftershock—and with Lance's father, Tate
O'Brien, a most enticing captor himself.

#572 LOOK BEYOND THE DREAM—Noelle Berry McCue
Erin Kennedy was surprised to land a job at a California health
club—and when she met her blue-blooded boss, Logan Sinclair, she
knew her wildest dreams had come true.

#573 TEMPORARY HONEYMOON—Katherine Granger
Overefficient Martha Simmons was just doing her job when she
agreed to temporarily marry her boss, Jake Molloy. But once they
said their "I dos," she hoped permanent love would follow.

#574 HOT ON HER TRAIL—Jean Barrett
Beth Holland was hiking the Appalachian Trail to save precious land
from destruction. Opposition came in the form of sexy Brian
McArdle.... Could he sidetrack Beth *and* walk away with her heart?

#575 SMILES—Cathie Linz
Classy dentist Laura Peters was haunted by fears of failure—until she
met roguish Sam Mitchell, who taught her to believe in herself and to
smile her doubts away.

#576 SHOWDOWN—Nancy Martin
Manhattan attorney Amelia Daniels came to Montana to find her
runaway daughter and ended up in the arms of June's *Man of the
Month*, charming, irascible cowboy Ross Fletcher!

AVAILABLE NOW:

A duo by Laurie Paige

There's no place like home—and Laurie Paige's delightful duo captures that heartwarming feeling in two special stories set in Arizona ranchland. Share the poignant homecomings of two lovely heroines—half sisters Lainie and Tess—as they travel on the road to romance with their rugged, handsome heroes.

A SEASON FOR HOMECOMING—Lainie and Dev's story…coming in June.

HOME FIRES BURNING BRIGHT—Tess and Carson's story…coming in July.

Come home to A SEASON FOR HOMECOMING and HOME FIRES BURNING BRIGHT…only from Silhouette Romance!

HB-1